WENDY J. FOX

WHAT IF
WE WERE
SOMEWHERE ELSE

STORIES

20 YEARS sf**WP**)

sfwp.com

Stories from this collection have appeared in or are forthcoming from:

Book of Names, a Spreadsheet *Rougarou*; When You Talk About the Weather, *Ragazine*; The Old Country, *Crack the Spine*; Pivot–Table; *Four Way Review* (published as Pivot); The Circle, *Blue Earth Review*; Tornado Watch, *Euphony*; The Empathy Chart, *Bayou Magazine*; Wish in the Other, *Paragon Press*; Pivot–Feather; *Broad River Review*; The Center of the Circle, *FRiGG*; More Terrible Ways to Make a Living, *Apricity Magazine*

Library of Congress Cataloging-in-Publication Data
Names: Fox, Wendy J., author.
Title: What if we were somewhere else : stories / Wendy J. Fox.
Description: Santa Fe, NM : Santa Fe Writers Project, [2021] | Summary:
"What If We Were Somewhere Else is the question everyone asks in these
linked stories as they try to figure out how to move on from job losses,
broken relationships, and fractured families. Following the employees of
a nameless corporation and their loved ones, these stories examine the
connections they forgee and the choices they make as they try to make
their lives mean something in the soulless, unforgiving hollowness of
corporate life. Looking hard at the families to which we are born and
the families we make, What If We Were Somewhere Else asks its own
questions about what it means to work, love, and age against the
uncertain backdrop of modern America"—Provided by publisher.
Identifiers: LCCN 2020047716 (print) | LCCN 2020047717 (ebook) |
    ISBN 9781951631055 (trade paperback) | ISBN 9781951631062 (ebook)
Classification: LCC PS3606.O97 A6 2021 (print) | LCC PS3606.O97 (ebook) |
    DDC 813/.6—dc23
LC record available at https://lccn.loc.gov/2020047716
LC ebook record available at https://lccn.loc.gov/2020047717

Published by SFWP
369 Montezuma Ave. #350
Santa Fe, NM 87501
(505) 428-9045
sfwp.com

To everyone who didn't let the door hit them in the ass on the way out.

CONTENTS

THE BOOK OF NAMES, A SPREADSHEET

In our office, there were sounds. One of the sounds was like a fighter plane taking off, the abrupt swirling of violent winds, the whoosh of air being displaced, but we all knew it was only the HVAC, which we pronounced in what we believed to be the expert way, *H-vack*, and so we did not worry about it in particular, we only complained. Indeed, the thermostat was an ongoing source of tension between us and the faces of the building maintenance crew, Barry and Terry. (We called them Berry and Tarry.) To them, depending on the season, we moaned of aching with heat or withering under cold.

We pay on the lease, and so we have the right to climate control, we said, and they nodded, and fiddled with the thermostat, and crawled into the ductwork while we typed.

We were perplexed at why it was so complicated. When we were in our own homes, we did not have this problem. We were able to adjust the temperature up or down to meet our whims, respond to cool weather with a pleasant wave of warmth, or to our night sweats with a blast of properly directed cold, smelling prettily of Freon. Yet, in the office, they worked regularly above us or in the mechanical room on the other side of us, their shared ladder like a bread crumb in a trail that would help them to find their way out from the innards of the building. The rattling of their wrenches, their urgent hammering, and their muffled swears could not rival the sounds of our fingertips on our keyboards.

The building was old and so some of the vestibules and corridors, we learned, were meant to be safe spots, built to function as a tornado shelter or to resist a bomb. Both weather and war were different when Denver's oilmen's club had raised the funds for the structure that eventually became our building. Their fourteenth-floor lounge was now a co-working space. And while we were not sure the aging construction could withstand cyclone or drone, they, the first owners, must have believed when the building was the tallest standing under Colorado's big sky, that they were immune to bad luck because unlike hotels and apartments, they had included a floor thirteen.

One of my employees, Melissa, took the stairs every day, all the way to our place on the twelfth floor, because she was young and fit, hiking the stories with her gazelle legs and her curtain of curly hair. We all envied her slim thighs.

Business suddenly got very good. We doubled, and then doubled again. We put some desks against the backs of cubes and in our interior hallway. We had never done anything special, like decorate with inspirational posters or corporate graffiti, and after we crammed desks up against the wall and then added chairs and people, we noticed the nice side effect of mitigating unproductive queuing for the microwave.

Our operations were lean and our staff prolific, and for this we congratulated ourselves during the all-hands company update meetings. Our CFO, for one, was frugal. For example: she got her lunch packets at a grocery outlet, a month's worth at a time, and her towers of low-fat chicken with broccoli and mild tandoori rice with chickpeas took up most of the freezer. If anyone was sore about it, they never said so. She had set an example by offering to accommodate two more desks in what had been her own private office, and we heard she was a good workmate—she brought snacks and didn't take too many phone calls.

Still, we ran out of room and people who we assumed were the colleagues of B & T scheduled a demolition—*demo*, we called it, new authorities in construction lingo—and when we returned on Monday morning, one wall had been cut away to reveal another office space with the same white paint and same gray carpet—but smaller, like a fraternal twin who had gotten the bad half of the genes—with only a half row of cubicles and even greasier whiteboards. Though the furniture and decor were identical, it was empty of any evidence of recent work, and a fine layer of powdered gypsum that had sprayed from the contractor's sawing of the drywall coated everything. It wasn't the posh designs of the original oilmen, but it worked for us.

One thing that we all liked was that the demo had revealed a backup kitchenette for the microwave, complete with a tiny dorm fridge. One of us said we should put beer in it, like college, but no one ever put beer in it.

Along with Melissa, and Michael, and Sabine, we had a new COO, Dave. He was a raw vegan, and he also did not eat gluten or soy or nightshades. He loved filtered water. He did not drink alcohol, of course, because of its dangerous properties, but also because of the sugar. I only knew nightshades from fairy tales, but when I looked it up, I found peppers and tomatoes were in this category. We were okay with him because he was not jumping the queue for the microwave (because he frowned on the microwave). He put bananas and apples and oranges in the candy bowl on the reception desk, but the administrative assistant was very good at her job, and because no one was eating the fruit, each day Rachel, the admin, removed one or two pieces from the dish and discarded it in the ladies' restroom, where the COO would not see it. I was concerned this was only attracting more roaches, but I complimented her on her thoughtfulness anyway. She kept the remaining candy in the dish at an even level, so it looked like no one had been touching it, even though she refilled the dish by the handful several times a day from a bag that the CFO had gotten on a trip to the grocery outlet.

At this time, things were not going well for me at home. I had a husband, and my husband was yelling at me—*Yes, you are yelling; no, you are not* just saying, *you are* yelling; *can't you hear yourself?*—about my mood when I came home from the office, and the piles of whiskey and wine bottles collecting by the recycling—*So take out the fucking recycling*, I would think, but I would not say it, I would only shrug about the piles of clinking glass and about everything.

Even though I was on the other side of the office, the miniature side, everything felt larger. Melissa's earbuds loomed, a bloom of creamy polycarbonate. The clatter of last night's dishes and the filmy leftovers of half and fully articulated fights felt like curtains on rails too tacky to draw.

A low hum started to permeate the office, and the conference room had a quality like old television sets being powered up or down—there was the sense of a frequency. Like a tube radio, Roger, the accountant whose father collected them, said of the interior corridor. In many of the cubicles, it was less vintage electronic and more preindustrial commerce, the muted snorting of horse breath and the muffled stamping of hogs. At least that is what I thought I heard.

In those days, B & T were even more challenged, with one side of the office polar and the other equatorial. We all noticed that the place the wall was removed was perfect, a conjunction of temperature zones. Yes, a bit gusty at the exact point where the two currents met, but certainly not unpleasant. Both my heavy knits and gauzy dresses seemed to fit here, and we started to hold meetings in the convergence zone to accommodate both sides of the office, and here, too, was where the hum was the least noticeable. We could hear it on either side of us, but at the seam, it was quiet.

Heather, our most talented analyst, had moved a portable, freestanding screen and positioned it in front of a projector. Once I had asked her if she thought I should keep growing my bangs or keep them short, and she made a spatial model of how it would impact me over time, and showed me how I had the potential for a neck injury, because I already had the habit of tossing my head to get the just barely too-long fringe out of my eyes. Heather was a *risk* analyst. "Don't cut," she had said.

Christian from IT added power strips and an Ethernet cord, and I did not contribute, other than to pantomime approval and ask Melissa to tidy up after the meetings, which she did not do, so I collected the scraps of paper and used coffee cups myself.

On the day my husband served me with divorce papers, the COO announced the official contraction. He said the markets had slowed, and that we had been somewhat untrue to our original governing policies and had grown too quickly. Heather had a chart that looked on one end like a highly manicured lawn and on the other, a lake full of milfoil.

It was our last meeting, and then those who had been on the list— Melissa, Michael, Tabatha, Mariette, Brian, Julie, Christian, Laird, Jorge, Dwayne, D'Shawn, Sabine, Trung, Roger, and Sommer—packed their desks into bankers boxes and rode the elevator down one last time, though Melissa, because she always took the stairs, said on her way out that it would be her first time.

Occasionally, I'd meet some of the fired employees for drinks, though never Heather, and I would tell them that the wall had been put back up, this time in brick, for ambiance, and the hum had stopped on the same day as the firings, and also, there had been more firings. We were back down to a half dozen, and the office was very quiet.

The H-vack was still a troubler, I said, but we weren't spending too much time on it. We were trying to grow.

WHEN YOU TALK ABOUT THE WEATHER

You and I are at a party somewhere, and first we have to talk about the weather, because we live in Denver, Colorado, where the skyline is unsettled and the temperature swings in wide dramatic swaths. Residents take some pride in it, even. *I was wearing shorts and sandals yesterday, and today this!* they say. (A scarf is tossed dramatically across a fuzzy cap, boots are stomped, snow shaken from a puffy vest; there is laughter.)

You, like nearly everyone who lives here, are an amateur weather person. At the party, when we hear the wind picking up outside, you have a gentle look, a *don't worry* look.

"It's coming from east," you say. "I don't think it will snow. And conditions aren't right for hail, so that's good news."

I tell you that I am not concerned about snow. It's May, so snow is possible, of course. Historically there has been snow in May, but mostly I don't worry about what I cannot control, mostly I do not give these things time.

At this party, we're both a few steps removed from the host, and whomever we have respectively come with has gone off to hide in the bathroom, or simply never arrived, or is outside smoking cigarettes in rapid succession because it is quiet back by the garbage cans and the recycling, where the only interruptions are the flick of the lighter and an occasional barking dog.

"I don't smell Greeley, either," you say. Greeley, sixty miles north of Denver, is where the beef slaughterhouses are. Conventional wisdom says that if there is cow dung on the wind from Greeley, snow is coming. The smell of Commerce City, where the dog food factory is, visible from downtown, means rain.

We move on a bit, and we talk about work—that other, constantly unavoidable thing that surrounds us—and I tell you I work in an office with creaky plumbing and questionable ventilation, and you think this is quaint, and you say, *Oh, startups*, like you know something about it. You say *gig economy*. You say *maker culture*.

I am not participating in any of these tech trends, just working in a shitty office.

At my office job, I am a risk analyst, and I do beautiful things with numbers. *Yes*, I say, *beautiful*.

I tell you that we, the staff, try not to mind the accommodations—if not technically a startup, it is a growing company. I want to help it grow. You nod your head when I tell you this, and you probably think I am a little naïve, maybe money-hungry, but you don't say anything.

I tell you that my work life is not very calm, but I manage to apply a lot of order there.

You are an accountant, so I think you could get into my numbers talk, that we could find some consensus.

"I just think it's so much more of a true meritocracy in tech," you say.

"Maybe," I say. "I mean, people like to think that. I'm not sure it's true."

Now there are other people, whom neither you nor I are either with or not with—just people, in a loose circle—one originally from the

Eastern Plains who says how easy we have all had it in Denver, because the tornadoes never touch the ground. One from the mountains who had lived in a draw of trees savaged by pine beetle, the ground so dry and the forest so brittle her family did not dare to light the barbecue, and her father started smoking the pot he scored from the nearby commune inside, in case a breeze took even a small ember from his joint to the forest floor.

Urbanites now, their gardens have been tarped and tomatoes have been bagged.

The people whom you don't know and I don't know now work in the credit or energy market. They are far from their old outhouses and former heirloom gardens.

And you.

You do not understand these country people who have become market people. You do back-office work, so you are not acquainted with the way they talk, uncomfortable with how they do not cease to remind you how you are benefiting their work by keeping your lights on, by ensuring your mortgage goes through. Yes, you have graduated and maintain your CPA, but you are young enough to still think that these onlookers will be interested in your stories from college. They are not.

These people are making money, and this is why they can afford a second round of red mulch when the first is destroyed in a spate of freezing rain.

You are trying to be polite—I *see* you trying to be polite—but you are wondering why they care about mulch so much, so much to do it twice. You live in a townhouse.

"I mean, if I had a yard," you say, "people would think they could bring their dogs over."

I can see you at work, your only slightly rumpled suit, your naturally stylish hair—it is tall and full in a way that is unanticipated but also not contrived—I can see you arguing about rev rec, making references to GAAP that no one else is interested in.

While the market people gab, I am admiring the fizz of my drink. I'm not a scientist, but I know that effervescence is the escape of gas from an aqueous solution, and the foaming or spraying that results is from release.

In my numbers work, I am given sheep by these market people and am expected to deliver a sweater—shear the beast, comb the thread, dye the fibers, spin the wool, knit it neatly and quickly and in the right size.

I told you, beautiful things.

*

We never find the people whom we were supposed to have come with, but we've stayed as the party dwindles. We are on a sofa, now that the bodies have thinned out and there are some places to sit, and I am starting to like something about you, but I don't know exactly what it is, and this is rocky terrain for me. I want to be enamored of the precise color of your shirt or the exact timbre of your voice or the specific way you hold your glass, but it's cloudier.

"Wait, so what do you really do, like in the everyday," you say. You're a little drunk, but I don't mind.

"I work with data," I say. I've moved on to wine, and I take a sip. "What kind of data?"

I try to give you the sheep and sweater analogy, but it's not making sense because I'm a little drunk as well.

"What kind of data," I repeat back to you. "Depends," I say. "What do you want to know?"

*

All across the Colorado foothills, clouds boiled or sliced with sun are either obscured by dust or pierced by spires and crags of rock, whether covered with perpetual snow or blazed with light. It's spring still, so there is a white-orange light in the northwest, a rainbow in the direct east, and a dull eggplant blue to the south. Hail will come or it will not. Like you, I live in a townhouse without a yard, and I pull my potted plants off the balcony to be prepared. A friend says I should stop doing this and that I should let my begonias and peppers and sunflowers toughen up.

For my part, I'm tired of toughness—I want some blooms. Pollen and volunteers. In the early season, I spilt a whole packet of New Mexico pepper seeds into dirt thinking only a few would come up, and suddenly I've got more seedlings than is reasonable.

I think about texting you to ask if you ever grow vegetables or herbs on your own balcony, and I think how this would be an interesting little data point, us eating the same fruit from the same origin, even if we are in two different places.

The flowers self-pollinate, so they're not hard to take care of, I almost type.

Instead, I send a message to my work group, @denveroffice, and ask who wants some starts. I thin and replant the seedlings into nursery containers. The work doesn't take long, and it is as tidy as any professional job, the little shoots sitting in freshly soaked soil.

My husband, Matt, asks me why I didn't just put them in the compost, not that he approves of the compost.

"I grew them from seed," I say.

"You can't compost if it came from a seed?"

"That's not the point," I say.

He says he thinks this seems like a lot of work, just to give something away, and I say I think it's a lot of work just to let something die.

*

I'm a pretty lucky person, for as much as I believe in luck, which is not all that much, but many are unluckier than I am. I mean luck like I never worked in the slaughterhouse or the dog food factory, those places I only smell.

When you went home, after we were out of party conversations, when the drinking and eating had run out of shine, and after I grabbed a taxi and you hitched a ride with a sober-ish person, you must have fallen back onto your pillow and thought, *God, that woman was weird.*

You sleep me off. By the time your coffee perks to done in the morning, you barely remember me.

It's when you're doing something small, like drying your hair that you'll flash a little.

You work the gel in. Or a plumping spray (you are contemporary, after all). In the rest of your grooming, you use a whitening toothpaste, an acne serum you have splurged on.

There's so much to know in the pattern of ritual, so much shape in these little facts, your cinnamon shampoo and your wheat bagels.

At the party, you gave me your number, even though I could see you trying to decide if you wanted me to call or not. You gave it to me because I asked, but you didn't ask for mine back. It didn't bother me. You didn't understand that I am incapable of letting numbers have no action.

And I call you. I call you three weeks later and I identify myself, and it will take you a moment to remember who I am, and then I will hear a sound like an office door clicking and you will say, *Sure, yes, of course.* And I will invite you for coffee and you will agree, but when we meet after work in the coffee shop, we will see that they also have cocktails, and so instead of java we split a bottle of wine, and it's not until close to the end that you notice my ring (I never take it off, just a slim silver band) and you say, *Wait, are you married?*

"I am," I say.

"Heather," you say, "Okay, that's fine, I just thought this was something different."

"You were right," I say. "You weren't wrong."

What you don't know, because you don't know me, is that I have already calculated what's at stake for me here. You are worried, but I am not.

What do you want to know?

*

Once, my boss and I got along, but by the time I meet you, we do not. Once, Kate and I had been very close, but Kate was going through a divorce. Kate was not doing very well.

At home, Matt and I, we are also not doing well. I lack empathy for Kate at work, but it is because I see how close I am to her. I put my life next to hers on a scatter chart, and I do not like the outcome. Too much correlation.

Kate asks me one day if she should cut her hair. Bangs, maybe, she says.

"No," I say. "Bangs can be risky, you know, you don't like your hair in your face, you'll be whipping your head around all the time, you'll hurt your neck." I've made this up entirely, but she seems to believe me. She gets a haircut and some awkward highlights, but no bangs.

In the house where I live with my husband, there is no diagram that can help me make sense.

You haven't heard any of this yet. I haven't told you because I don't want you, or anyone, to know so much about me.

If you asked me what I wanted to know, at the party, or at the coffee shop date, I would have said, *Courage. I need to know how to find courage.*

My husband is fine, actually, but he was a hedge. He was young, I was very young, and despite knowing the statistics, I donned an ecru dress—you might not know this color, but it is the light beige of unbleached silk or linen—and stumbled down the aisle, gardenias and lilies and hydrangeas blazing white on the sides. My mother, in café au lait; his mother, draped in eggshell and putty. Our fathers, matching in navy.

A decade and a half later, we have no children, a flagging commitment, and a lot of ice in the freezer. Matt does not like to run out of ice.

There are many things Matt does not like.

Matt does not like seafood.

Matt does not like wrinkled sheets.

Matt does not like coffee, nor the smell of coffee.

Matt does not like me anymore, I am fairly sure.

Matt would certainly not like you.

There are some things that Matt does like. For example, he likes his job. He slogs long hours, and there was a time I thought it was just to be away from me, but it is simply him, and I don't fault him for it. This is a first marriage for both of us.

You call me at work because I have given you my desk line.

"Are you free today?" you want to know. It has been seven days, Thursday to Wednesday.

"I can make something up," I say.

"Same place?"

We meet at the coffee shop that has cocktails, and we get a bottle of wine again, though this time it turns into two, and the barista is mopping up, and I think that we should go. We're not drunk so much as glowing.

"Come over to my place," you say. "It's not far."

"Not yet," I say, because there is this blur that is not working for me, the part of you that I cannot quite parse, where I can't tell if it's something real or only something new.

*

The office I work in has become very crowded, and the close proximity and the dull whine of so many laptops running, the ticking of keyboards being typed on—a sound like an inconsistent rain—is stressing the staff. I read that when chickens are crammed too many to one pen, they'll begin to peck one another's eyeballs out and we do. There are fights over stolen lunches, there are endless complaints about the temperature, there is general malaise. We decide to expand into an adjoining space, and construction, or deconstruction, begins: a wall is being removed. The sound of sawing does not improve the general mood, but I try to remind the people whom I talk with that it will get better.

Kate, in particular, is unraveling. She says that removing the wall is a very bad idea. It's not so much that she believes there is something horrible on the other side of it, but more that there is a very delicate balance in the office and that by removing the wall we are upsetting it.

She asks me again if she should cut her hair. I think it is never a good idea to get haircuts in a poor mental state and tell her *No* again. *Your hair is fine,* I say, *and we already discussed your bangs.*

As soon as the construction dust has been cleaned up and we've rearranged the desks and gotten people settled into the new space, the markets begin to crash. A free fall.

Management says nothing. Management purchases a new microwave to relieve the bottleneck in the kitchen. Kate, who has always been an eclectic dresser, begins to show up in outfits that are truly strange. A miniskirt and mud boots. A suit jacket paired with a swimsuit cover-up meant to pass as a dress.

I check my own clothes. I'm feeling like Kate a little bit, but I think I am hiding it better, so far. Black pants and a white collared blouse. I could work at a grocery store, or a travel agency, or at a broker's office, or here.

*

I am given a project, the kind that is my specialty.

I map the productivity of every worker, their specific impact to revenue, and I start building it into a chart.

There are many factors. Michael in sales brings in revenue, but he also creates discord. He is the source of many lunch thefts, though no one but me would ever guess it was him. I wouldn't have guessed either, until I caught him. There is cost in these actions.

Sabine seems not specifically revenue-facing, but she also interacts with customers. Flirts with them on the phone or over e-mail. She's likeable, she's sticky.

I am also building another chart, more like a graph. This one is for survivors, and it was not assigned, so I do it on my own time. This one helps them feel better after the layoffs inevitably come. It shows their productivity. It emphasizes efficient use of time. When the layoffs are finalized, I will bring out this chart as a kind of salve. The workers will say, *But we could have done better*, and my chart will illuminate how they are wrong, even in this. HR would think this is a negative message, but facts do not operate positively or negatively.

Mostly, as I am working, I think of you. Our three meetings. Your comments about hail begin to feel like an allegiance. I think of the way you invited me over, and of the nitrogen smell of rain.

I think of my husband, and my office. I wonder what you want, and I wonder at the reality that I do not know what I want.

In all of my projects, there is missing data.

*

You call me on my desk line again. You have my home number, but you say you can't call me at home. It's the middle of the day, and you're taking lunch, and I try to remember the last time I left the office for lunch.

"I'm right by your building," you say. "Come down and have a coffee at least."

I am nervous to see you, maybe because it's daylight, but I say *Yes*, and I meet you outside of my building, and then we walk to our coffee shop, where we finally do have coffee, and we split a sandwich.

"But what about your husband," you whisper.

"You don't have to whisper," I whisper.

I try to tell you about the charts, and again about making sweaters for the market people.

"Can I see one of them?" you ask, meaning the charts, but I say no, it's too proprietary. You say that no one knows you in my office, and I say it doesn't matter.

I do want to show you one of the charts, but they are not ready yet. Right now, there are only numbers in columns and pivot tables. I'm still in the discovery phase. I dig, I organize. It's like gardening with unmarked seeds, but there are a few little blooms in the numbers here and there. About half of my pepper starts have disappeared from the kitchen—off to good homes, I hope—and the others are wilting hopelessly, unable to feed on fluorescents.

"So how come you see me if you're married," you say.

I think you must know how much I love specific questions, and I think I must know how much you love specific answers.

We've not touched yet, besides an awkward brush here or there, so I reach for your hand across the table, and our fingers link.

You ask me if I remember at the party the energy people, and I say that of course I do, but that I call them market people, *Not that the nomenclature matters*, I say. You ask me if I remember how proud they were of their success stories. I realize you understand more than I thought.

Outside the weather has shifted from a bright June day to the beginnings of an afternoon thunderstorm. The air has gone gray, and there are bits of trash swirling in the wind.

In two weeks, I will hand in my productivity chart to management, and most of the office will be let go. That afternoon, I will stand where the wall was removed, and I will present my other chart to the remaining employees.

I will go home that evening, and Matt will make dinner.

I will sit on my patio with a glass of wine and admire the blooms on my peony, the fire of the celosia.

For now, our fingers touch as you eye the skyline.

There's a lot that I want to say to you, about Matt, about work, about trying to answer my question, about answering your question.

"It will probably stay nice for the rest of the day," you say. I am not worried about the weather.

THE OLD COUNTRY

In my life then, in high school with my best friend, Cale, I'd say that there was this layer of not-caring-ness. Like in the videos of birds hatching we watched in biology. It's the spot where the chick has started to bust through the shell, but is still encased in the membrane, the grossest part, wet feathers wriggling under a layer of collagen. It's like Cale's face when we used to play bank robbers and we'd stuff our heads into my mom's old pantyhose.

From underneath the nylon, I could sort of see everything but not make out anything, and while the chicks eventually emerged from the egg, it felt like Cale and I were still there, half in and half out, just one tear away from emerging as our full selves, wet and briny and wide-eyed, like if we just reached a little harder, like there was something more to reach toward.

*

Cale and I were in his dad's basement. He had just told me that his dad had said my mom was "smoking hot," and I wasn't sure if I was supposed to pass this information on to my mom or what, so I passed him the bong to try to shut him up.

"I think she's pretty hot too, dude," Cale said, flicking his lighter. He took a long inhale as the water bubbled in the chamber and then he pulled the stem that held the bowl to exhaust the rest of the smoke. "I mean, I guess I hadn't really thought about it until Dad said something and then I was like, *yeah*, totally, *Mrs. D. is a MILF.*"

"Nobody calls my mom Mrs. D.," I said.

"I just did." He passed the bong back.

"She isn't a missus, you know. She's not married. Her name is Linda. You know that," I said.

Cale and I talked a lot, but we didn't talk about the part of what held us together, which was that both of our parents were divorced. Once in a while, we did things all together, my mom and me with his dad and him, and I think Cale and I both had the same secret hope our parents would fall in love and we would be real brothers. I remember once when the four of us went to a movie, we were sitting in between my mom and his dad, and Cale said something about how we needed to sit on the end, so we moved around until our folks were next to each other. I nodded and he nodded back, but that was as close as we ever got to acknowledging it.

"How old is your mom, anyway," Cale said. "I mean, other than old enough."

"Stop it," I said. We talked like this about women sometimes, but I didn't like it. "I promise you, you are not losing your virginity to my mother."

"Probably true," Cale said. "Hey, give me my lighter."

The two of us didn't really have other friends. We weren't unpopular, we were just gliding through high school, trying to stay invisible. Cale was very good at math, I was very good at English, and we traded our homework around so we were B+ average. I'm sure our teachers knew—we weren't exactly savvy—but like all the other adults around us, there was that gloss of indifference.

*

The thing about my mom was that she gave me this traditional name, Laird, and she must have thought I'd live up to it. I was all the way in high school before I learned that a laird was someone who owned a large estate. Not Laird, a laird. It's like naming your kid Esquire, though it also translates to Lord. I knew other people had this name, but I still always thought it was dumb, though my mom said that she didn't appreciate me being so negative toward her vision for me.

Her vi*sion* was the way she pronounced it.

It made sense, I guess. We were just on the cusp of girls named Nevaeh—heaven spelled backward, though I wondered, wouldn't the backward of "heaven" be "hell"?—and boys with newly edgy old-timey Bible names like Jedidiah and Zebulon, so Cale and I didn't feel too misplaced. Cale was the Misspelled Vegetable; I was the Lord of Nothing.

My mom and I had the same last name, which was not the same last name as my father.

Also, I don't think we were Scottish—or if we were, we weren't doing anything with it. I mean, we didn't talk about our clans or trace our ancestry or take a trip and call it visiting the "old country." It was rare that we'd go anywhere, but if we did, we'd drive to Arizona or southern California. We went to places that were predictably warm, predictably dry. Usually it was just me and her visiting friends of hers, though once in a while there'd be a boyfriend around.

We didn't really talk about my dad. He'd been gone a long time.

There was one guy, a redhead who, when I was in my earliest teens, started coming around and then he seemed to resurface a lot. For a while I tried to pretend he was my father, even though he was quite a bit younger than my mom, but mom was young, too. She was only twenty when she had me.

I never knew exactly what her vi*sion* was or what it was supposed to mean, and I didn't ask. She didn't say much about it, except when I complained.

I even thought the redhead and my mom would stay together, but then he hadn't been at our house for a couple of months, and when I mentioned it to Mom, she said she was done with him.

"Why?" I asked. I had liked him, in a way. I had liked him because it seemed like he made her mostly happy, and selfishly, because he was nice to me. I guess I hadn't thought about how he might get in the way of her marrying Cale's dad. Sometimes the redhead would slip me a twenty, and the summer that I was fifteen and a half and had my learner's permit, he let me practice driving in his Honda. Which seemed very normal, I thought, a Honda. My mother drove a Grand Am, which might have been a nice car in the nineties sometime, seemed sporty, but now it was trying too hard to hang onto being cool.

"He got married, you know," she said. "To his ex. She has some fancy job downtown. We'll see if that lasts," she snorted.

I wasn't sure if my mom meant the job or the marriage, but in any case, it was a long time before I saw the redhead again.

*

When Cale and I were juniors in high school, we spent most of our time looking for dope. We smoked pot, mostly, because it was the easiest and the cheapest to get, but we preferred acid, mushrooms. At least that's what we told each other.

"Dude," Cale said after school one Friday, "there's a party at Jordan Johnson's house, and I heard there'll be 'shrooms."

"I don't have any money," I said.

"No worries," Cale said. "I got you."

Cale's allowance was much larger than mine. Meaning, Cale had an allowance.

There were plenty of single parents in our school, but Cale had the only single dad. To hear him tell it, his mother had run off with some dickbag, a real piece of shit, and even if she wanted to come home, they were not going to let her.

Another thing we didn't talk about was that my dad was that dickbag, that real piece of shit. Cale's actual biological mom didn't leave with my actual biological dad, just a guy like him. My mom and I, we would have said the same thing about him coming home—that we changed the locks and all that. And we really did.

My mother, kneeling at the door, hardware spread out around her.

Just being smart, my mom had said.

It was evening, early, but I think I was in pajamas.

We live in a rental house, and you never know how many keys are floating around, she said.

I don't remember so much about him, but I don't remember nothing. It wasn't dramatic when he left. One day he was there, and the next day he wasn't. I had this cereal bowl with a bear's face in the bottom of it that I really liked, and sometimes he'd use it for an ashtray. One of the bear's eyes was burned out, but I still ate from it.

I was definitely in pajamas, because I remember the way the footies squished against the vinyl floor.

If your father wants to come inside, he'll need to act right. He's not just barging in. He has to knock.

My mother, her hair pulled back, worked the old latch and the deadbolt out of its groove, then put the new one in place. She was following the instructions on the package, and I could see her trying very hard to be patient, trying very hard to stay calm.

I was her helper. The face on my bear cereal bowl would keep his other eye.

I was warm in my pajamas.

Later I realized that a lot of people would have called someone, like a locksmith or a landlord, to come out and do this, or if they were doing it themselves, they would have tools instead of a butter knife as a flathead screwdriver and a can opener as a wrench.

I held the new screws in my outstretched hand.

*

There were no mushrooms at Jordan Johnson's party. I'm not saying we didn't have fun. Actually, I was a little glad. The only time Cale and I had done mushrooms before, we could only get about half of a very small stem and a tiny cap with what was left of his allowance, and so we traded the piece of shrivel back and forth between us, licking it until it was just kind of soggy, like cardboard that held an over-used Tootsie Pop.

We swallowed what was left of the stem after it fell apart in my hands.

I'm not sure if we got high, but I know we were tired—we'd stayed up too late, being too careful with the cap.

"Hey, I think I see something," Cale said, just as I was dozing off.

"Is it blue?" I said.

"It's totally blue," he said. "A bright, perfect blue."

"I think that's your dad's bug lamp," I said.

"Right on," Cale said, and his breathing collapsed into snores.

*

One thing I remember is that after my mom changed the locks, she was at the peephole all the time. She'd hear something and ask me if I heard it, but I never heard anything. Had that been part of her *vision*? I wasn't sure.

I was also getting very tired of my pajamas. I wanted to go to school. I wanted to eat my cereal from the bear bowl and brush my teeth and put on my jeans and hop on the bus.

Like Mom *used* to say, "Get out there and hop on the bus, Lairdy."
When I asked about going to school, she said I needed to wait.

"He could be watching," she said.

I didn't think he was watching, and Mom definitely wasn't watching me. I knew where the washcloths were, so I washed my face and brushed my teeth. I got dressed, and I put my pajamas in the clothes hamper. I took my books from my backpack and spread them on the kitchen table, thinking of my teacher and my desk. I put my cereal in the bear bowl. There was no milk, so I ate it dry.

"What are you doing?" she asked.

"School," I said. I still had dry cereal stuck in my teeth, and I was working it out with my tongue.

"I'm so proud of you, Laird," she said.

"Thank you," I said. One piece of generic wheat loop came loose.

I wanted to tell her I didn't know where to start in my workbook, but she was already back at the peephole, so I flipped to a random page.

*

The thing about my mom was that she was okay, eventually. One day I woke up and she had my lunch pail and clean pants and she was rushing me out the door, and it was *Hop on the bus, Lairdy!* again.

I was nervous about showing up, but it turns out missing three weeks of the second grade is not the worst thing. Mom went back to work. The peephole stayed undarkened. We didn't talk about it.

Years later, when the redhead left, I asked if we were going to change the locks, and she said, *Wait, what? Um, no.*

*

In fact, I wasn't sure what my mother's *vision* was at all, for herself, or for me. We stayed in the same house; she worked the same job. I hung out with Cale; she hung out with ladies from her office—she was an administrative assistant, and even now I correct someone who says "secretary." *Show a little respect*, I'll say. *Unless you are talking about the Secretary of State or something, it's* administrative assistant, *seriously.*

I think my mom would have really liked to have a daughter. The one time I took a girl to a dance, she asked if Brianna could come over beforehand.

"Maybe I could do her makeup?"

"I don't think so, Mom. That's weird."

But I guess I was wrong because when I told Bri about it later, when I was trying to help her understand that I didn't get weird all on my own, she said she thought it was sweet. She said, *Hey, have your mom call me anytime. I would totally get a pedi with her*, but I didn't tell my mom anything about that.

It's not like Brianna ever called me back after that one dance, anyway.

*

"Guys, I need you to keep the windows open down there if you are going to be smoking in the basement," Cale's dad said. "I really don't care, but be a little more conscientious, you know?"

Once, Cale's dad had told me to call him by his first name, Kevin, but I didn't want to call him Kevin.

"Yeah, but we're not really *smoking*, Dad," Cale said.

"No? Then why does the basement smell like a skunk? Enlighten me."

"It's more like, I mean, not to put too fine a point, but technically we're more like taking massive bong rips," Cale said.

"That involves smoke," his dad said, "that you inhale into your lungs and then exhale, which is smoking. Technically."

"Whatever, man, you're the engineer," said Cale.

It was true. Cale's dad was an engineer. He was kind of a dork, but I understood how that could be cool once you weren't in high school anymore. Like, Cale's dad wouldn't even need to call a locksmith because he had his own tools. Cale's dad probably knew how to make a key from a wax mold or whatever professional lock people did.

"What do you think, Laird? Smoking or not smoking?"

This was supposed to be the place where I could shine and use a word like *nomenclature* or *colloquialism*. Instead, I made a dumb kind of pun and I said, "All I know is I heard you think my mom is *smoking* hot."

Cale wouldn't meet my eyes, but his dad lifted an eyebrow.

"Back to the basement, guys. Keep the window open."

For the rest of the afternoon, we watched TV, being respectfully defiant, blowing our smoke out of the open window, exhaling through a toilet paper tube stuffed with dryer sheets.

*

When we were seniors, Cale got a scholarship because he was the one who was good at math. Our final year was horrible in that pantyhose-over-the-head way. We'd try to hang out and have fun, but I knew he was moving out of state and I was going to stay home and go to the community college, and every moment was punctured by the idea of him leaving.

Cale's dad said it didn't matter where anyone went, it only mattered what you did.

"You can still come over any time, Buddy," he said to me.

On the day Cale left for the dorms, I helped him load his stuff into the car and I kept wondering if I should tell him that I loved him, because I did really love him, but when he went to get in the passenger side, his dad already belted in, I didn't have words.

"Peace, dude," Cale said.

"Peace," I said.

We didn't hug or even shake hands or chest bump, not that we had ever chest bumped.

As the car pulled away from the house, I kept wondering what that sound was, *what was that horrible snorting sound*, until my mom pulled me in close to her and I realized it was me, crying and sniveling and really kind of freaking out.

"Oh, Lairdy Laird," she said. "I'm so sorry. This was not in the *vision*."

*

While Cale was at school, sometimes he and I would email, in a sentimental way.

Dear Lord of Nothing, he would write.

Hello, Misspelled Vegetable! I'd respond.

Once in a while, when he was back home for the holidays, we'd smoke pot in his dad's basement and we'd open the window, we'd fill a toilet paper tube with dryer sheets, and we'd be conscientious.

Cale talked about his classes—advanced geometry and trig. His lab partner in organic chem was a real shit, I learned.

"What are the girls like in junior college?" he asked.

"What did you say?" I hated that, *junior college*.

"At your school, what are the girls like."

"They're girls. I mean, not really girls. There are a lot of returning students, which is cool, in the mix." I hoped I sounded like I knew what I was talking about.

"So, they're easy?" Cale pulled the stem out of the bong, the way he always had.

"What?"

"Nothing, dude. It's just… Sorority chicks. You are missing out."

*

I actually really loved my community college. The instructors were kind. My peers had lives and homes, and some had kids of their own, and we were all working pretty hard. Cale had told me about massive lecture halls with hundreds of students, and I wasn't sure how that was better than a small classroom.

I did eventually transfer to a university, downtown, at the extension campus. By that time, Cale was already starting to think about master's and future PhD programs, and I was still living with my mom.

It will mostly come down to where I get funding, he said over email.

I wasn't sure what to say. I knew it wasn't cool to be a twenty-something guy and not have my own place, and I was taking a creative writing class, so I was definitely getting a more sophisticated understanding of cliché.

Of course, I wasn't planning on staying in my childhood room forever, but I liked being up early in our house. I'd go for a run in the filmy dawn and then make coffee for us both. My mom had always used cheap pre-ground in an electric percolator, but I used fresh beans and heated water for French press, and when it was just ready to pour, I tapped at her door. She'd come out, in her robe, and we'd have the coffee, and I'd poach eggs and make toast. A guy at school I hung out with sometimes had taught me about coffee, and the same guy had showed me how to make eggs.

I had tried to write about the mornings with my mom in my creative writing workshop, and I had tried again to write about it in an email to Cale, and both said it was some kind of Oedipal thing. I couldn't get on the page how it wasn't—it was more of a shift, a tear in the nylon, a snag in the membrane, to know my mom as an adult.

I mean, she was my mother and I was her son, and we had a lot of hard times after my dad left when she was scared and I was too young to do anything or even know how to do anything, and now that I was old enough, I just wanted to make my mother a nice cup of fucking coffee and a decent fucking breakfast and be kind to her because I was still working on how to say, *Hey, thank you for holding it together, that must have been really hard, I can't even imagine,* and the only way sometimes is to do some other kindness like the coffee and an egg on toast, and it doesn't take away what it would feel like to have an eyeball glued to the peephole for three terrified weeks while a child eats dry cereal from a bowl with a bear in the bottom with one eye burned out. But it is something. It was all I had to give, and I wanted to give it to her, every single day.

While Cale emailed less and less, he always asked how my mom was, and I wanted to say, *Dude, what are you doing for your dad? People get lonely, you know.* But I didn't.

In early summer, just before I graduated, I invited Cale's dad over for dinner. Maybe it was a last ditch of trying to hold the connection of our old fantasy of our folks falling in love. We had a good time. I made a roast and Kevin brought wine and we drank our way through a couple of bottles, but it was clear there was nothing between my mom and him, and never had been, besides me and Cale.

The dinner was an ending, and I wished my friend was there to see it.

*

Cale got his funding for a doctoral program, and I got a job in an office. I still wanted to write, but I knew it wouldn't pay. I started as a temp and then was hired full time. I had my own apartment then, and there were things I liked about it, but there were also times it seemed ridiculous, when I'd be sitting around by myself and my mom was sitting around by herself and we were probably both wondering what the point of the separation was while we stared at the wall.

At my office holiday party that first year, I was talking to my coworkers Heather, Sabine, and Michael, and I saw a flash of red hair.

"Who is that?"

"Jimmy," Sabine said. "Kate's husband."

Kate was our boss. Mom and I had always called that redheaded guy James, before he was my boss's husband, when he drove a Honda and slipped me twenties. Jaime, sometimes, but never Jimmy.

We were standing by the makeshift bar, a low table that had been set up near the copy machine.

"They're still together?" I asked.

"Barely," said Heather, taking a long drink. "At least to hear Kate tell it. I don't know. I try not to ask too much."

I wasn't sure then what to do, but I did start to understand my mother's vision. You have even a slightly unusual name and people won't forget it—he might have forgotten my face, and my face had changed in any case, but how many vaguely familiar guys named *Laird* could he really know.

"Hey, Heather, introduce me?" And she did.

We went outside so Jimmy could smoke. He said he was supposed to be quitting, but he was always looking for excuses. Like seeing someone from the past, he said as he lit up, that was a good enough excuse.

There was a feathering snow, but it wasn't too cold. We ducked under an awning, where there was a pretty glow of holiday lights.

"Who was that kid you were always so obsessed with," Jimmy said. "I always thought he was a punk, but Linda asked me not to say anything."

"Cale," I said. "He's doing a PhD in theoretical mathematics."

"And your mother?"

"She's well," I said. "But bored, I think."

"We're all bored," Jimmy said, smoke puffing out of his last syllable. "I missed her, you know, and I missed you."

I wasn't sure what to say. We looked around, as red and green flashed on the snow.

"I guess I didn't think I'd ever see you again," I said.

He nodded. When I blinked against the snow, it could have just as easily been Cale there, kicking at the ice near the curb.

"So, I think this is good," I said.

Jimmy nodded, though I couldn't tell if it was a yes or a no, and stamped out his cigarette.

The wind had shifted to feel like a bite, and I turned my collar up.

I knew I would tell my mother I'd seen him, and I was already thinking what I'd say.

He didn't look good, you know, like not bad or unhealthy, just... not happy.

I knew it, she'd say. *I knew it.*

And we would be having this conversation in the morning because I would have gotten up early to make it to my mom's place in time to make the coffee. I would have sent a text to Cale that he would probably never return, and on Monday I would go to work and see my boss, who was married to my mom's old boyfriend.

When the snow started swirling harder, Jimmy had gone back to the office party, and when I blinked, I was like the bear with the missing eye.

Lord of Nothing.

Her *vision*.

One perfect egg, on one perfect toast.

PIVOT, TABLE

In the office, coworkers Sabine and Michael sat quietly at their cubicles. In the office, there was flux. For example, sometimes the temperature waffled between tropical and arctic, and the managerial staff also ran hot and cold. Sabine sat with Michael on her right and Melissa, who had been hired before her and always wore earbuds, on her left. Their collective boss, Kate, was going through a divorce and sometimes had outbursts, and at these times Sabine and Michael turned toward their desktop screens. Melissa, through her earbuds, either did not hear or pretended not to.

Sabine had lied to get the job. She didn't know anything about making slide presentations or spreadsheets.

"How are your pivot tables?" Kate had asked in the interview. "You'll be cross-trained to support a woman named Heather, and she'll need this."

"Well, I think they usually turn out beautifully," Sabine had replied. Her response seemed to go over well, though she didn't really know what a pivot table was. It had to do with Excel, she knew that, but why or how? No clue.

It didn't matter to her, lying. She'd lied to get her last job, at a coffee shop. It was just a job. In that interview, she had said, *I prefer medium-body roasts with a strong finish*, when in fact she had no idea what she preferred. None of it was life or death. It wasn't like she was pretending to be a doctor.

The coffee shop had taken her roughly through college—she didn't actually graduate—and she had enjoyed working there. She liked learning how to properly grind the beans and then tamp the grounds. She enjoyed negotiating the old, fussy espresso maker, and she enjoyed pulling the shots into warm mugs. She did not enjoy steaming milk because she believed her coffee was good enough not to need milk, but she still steamed with aplomb, until the foam coated the back of a spoon. Occasionally, if she was hungry, she could admit that milk-steaming be damned, she did enjoy a very dry cappuccino.

After she dropped out and the semester turned and the coffee shop teemed with new freshmen, with their textbooks and their hope bonking against the regulars at their usual tables, she understood she couldn't stay because she wasn't either of them. She was their barista, not their peer.

On a break one day, Sabine used the community computer to begin contriving a résumé, inventing nearly all of its content. Besides the freshmen, she had two other groups of clientele: the consultants and the writers, and she drew her inspiration from them—from the consultants, a bullet-pointed skillset; from the writers, a sense of hope that if she could just get it down, the next line (always the *next* line) might be perfect enough to nudge her whole life forward.

Besides, it seemed like all the two groups ever did was type, and she could *touch* type. It was the writers she admired more. Some had a few published pieces, and all had books in various stages. She liked their dreaminess, the way they made it up as they went along, even if most of them tipped poorly.

And it was the writers who, when the city entertained zoning a chain coffee shop only a few blocks down, hosted a rally and showed up with pithy signs, and it seemed to work. The chain did not appear in the neighborhood. Maybe, even, Sabine's job was saved.

The coffee shop had responded by opening up for more readings. Instead of just the Tuesday open mic that had been a standard since well before Sabine's time, every other weeknight and alternating Fridays gave space to the writers, and so she heard the way they fabricated, and she heard the way they frequently could not separate these fabrications from their own lives.

She understood them a little more as she worked on the résumé, as the project stretched from just one break to two, to three, to a whole month of breaks. Sometimes she thought she was judging them a little harshly. At other times she thought if they would spend less time drinking coffee and smoking cigarettes, they'd get more writing done.

At their readings, their abundant, repetitive readings, the short-shorts and prose poems would echo from the cheap, poorly adjusted microphone and ping against the espresso machine, so that no matter how carefully they had constructed their sentences and stanzas, it all sounded like clatter. Sometimes she recognized the stories from her customers' lives, like the time Penelope (photo essays) and Raul (short-stories with an emphasis on temporalization) had ended their eight-year affair at the corner table, the best table, there by the window and overlooking the mountains (slideshow by Penelope, captions by Raul). There was the time Jane (nonfiction) and her teenage daughter Chrysanthemum (free verse, contemporary haiku, and hybrid poetry) thought they had been evicted, but it turned out to be okay; it was only that they were both stoned and were at unit 401 instead of their own 501, and they didn't understand right away, as their world filtered through a slow pot swirl, that the notice tacked to the door was not for them, because it was not their door, not their furniture inside when they jiggled the handle to get in so they could quickly round up what they could carry. The mauve sofa in 401 jolted them to realization—(verse and live gong by Chrysa, reading by Jane):

What a difference
Just one flight up those old stairs
Makes for us, Mother

Sabine thought of them as she used one of the built-in templates from the word processing software. She had started by putting her name and address at the top, but sometimes she retyped it. In fact, she had retyped it probably a hundred times, just so she could feel the action of her fingertips on the keyboard, to feel like she was working.

Of course, she had noticed the writers always changed what happened, trying for drama. The consultants probably did too. She didn't know what the consultants did at their jobs, but she saw the spreadsheets, the charts, and she had taken enough statistics, worked her butt off for a B- even, to understand that there was as much interpretation in data as in trouble and love.

Almost evicted.
(Cool blue light under the door)
My home. Mother's home.

And Penelope's Polaroid photos, grainy and off-color because she bought old, unpredictable film from eBay to save money and then coated the prints in Mod Podge to seal them up and scanned batches at the library, paired with Raul's minimalist narration, actually worked well, Sabine thought, but it was nothing like them as a couple. As a couple they did not have the gritty tension of mixed media. As a couple they were boring, and each had complicated coffee orders, and they argued about whether it was okay for Penelope to say she was vegetarian when she was actually pescatarian.

"Fish are animals too, Penelope," Raul would say.

"But no one knows what it *means*," Penelope would answer.

"I know what it means," Raul said.

"But you're *vegan*. Of course, *you* know. Most people consider eating only fish to be vegetarian."

In her time at the coffee shop, Sabine heard a hundred variations on this argument, and a hundred times she had assured Raul that she never put his almond milk into the dairy steamer, even though she did it all the time.

"Catholics maybe think this, the Lent thing, think they are giving up meat," Raul would say to Penelope, "but don't put your religious industrial complex in this space. Fish have eyeballs. Broccoli does not have eyeballs!"

And one series on their slides, during their reading/presentation, did address this. A corn with human ears. Eyes on potatoes, on beans. A radicchio styled to look like a vagina—Penelope's vagina. Kiwi fruit as Raul's balls, avocado as another man's larger balls.

By the time the readings started, the consultants were always gone. They finished work at two or three, snapping their laptop cases shut, packing up their messenger bags, and padding out into the street in their colored tennis shoes, headed to their condos for a night of Netflix or other Wi-Fi-enabled activities.

On the community computer, Sabine listed her college, and she listed her imaginary skillset.

She asked her boyfriend, who she shared an apartment with, to take a look, but he only shook his head and instructed her not to sell out. Later, she would ask Raul to proofread it and Penelope to offer some suggestions for design flair (lines at the side, Sabine's name in cerulean blue). Chrysa changed her objective so it read:

Making coffee now
But looking for my big break
Call, not pull, the shots?

It took Sabine longer to ask one of the more regular consultants to take a look, and while she didn't know a thing about him besides his coffee order (doppio) she believed that he would offer her the ruthless critique she needed.

"Too many words, too much color," he said, while looking at his phone. "Sentences aren't helpful. Just use bullets and tabs. Everything has to be tracked back to a result," he said. "And listen, what's your number? I'll text you a list of words you have to work in."

"I have a pen," Sabine said.

"I'd rather text," he said.

She recited her number, and he sent the text, and she stared at it for a while. *Velocity. Synergy. Demonstrable. Actionable. Ecosystem.*

"Okay," she said. "Thank you."

At the community computer, she deleted Chrysa's objective, Penelope's blue lines, and Raul's semicolons. She did so a little guiltily, ignoring the advice of all the people she liked best.

Demonstrable experience in enabling synergy with actionable approach to departmental velocity. Deep experience with complicated ecosystems.

"Good," the consultant said.

"I don't even know what that means."

"That's fine. Meaning isn't really the point. It's not art, it's just a résumé. I'll text you a couple of places I know are hiring."

She submitted. Then she waited. Then, to her surprise, she got calls.

*

At the first interview, she did very poorly. She was dressed wrong, and her hair looked messy.

She showed up at the coffee shop and the consultant was there, and his face fell.

"Is that what you wore?" he asked. "It's okay. I'll text you some images of serious-interview-casual," he said.

That night he stayed until almost closing and Sabine understood he was waiting on her. He wasn't bad looking, and he was helpful.

She reminded herself of this later when she was in his loft and he was pounding happily away on top of her. She tried to conjure Penelope and construct haiku in her head to make the time pass, but it didn't last long enough for her to get beyond the first stanza

He is helping you—

For the second interview, Sabine blow-dried. Her head felt bouncy, and when paired with the gray twinset she'd found at a secondhand store, she thought she could pass for the type of person who held a desk job. Her boyfriend said she looked like her mother.

"What's your greatest weakness?" the second interviewer asked.

Sabine correctly recognized this as a place where she should tell a lie. "My greatest weakness is that I am sometimes too truthful," she said.

"Can you relate that characteristic to this role?"

"No," Sabine said. "I cannot."

"Okay," the interviewer said. "Well, that's truthful, but not really what I'm looking for."

On the third interview, with Kate (nervous, distracted Kate), Sabine wore the twinset, blow-dried, and texted the consultant beforehand. *What do I do if I don't know the answer to a question? Dodge,* he replied. *Just make some shit up.*

"How are your pivot tables?" Kate asked.

"Well, I think they usually turn out beautifully," Sabine replied.

When she got the offer, she was shocked at the salary, at the number of vacation days. Health *and* dental *and* vision. She ran her tongue across her teeth and imagined how much smoother they would be with two annual cleanings. She squinted—she didn't need glasses, but she could get some anyway.

Her boyfriend was not impressed.

Her boyfriend's name was Ryan, but he preferred to go by Sebastian.

Sabine didn't care what he went by, since she'd spent her whole life having the pronounced *e* of her name dropped.

He was still piddling at school, in a studio program. The program was actually competitive, but Sabine honestly could not pick out his installation art from any of his peers'. At the shows, there was string, a lot of string, and there were nails and scraps of denim; there was salt everywhere, salt making the slick gallery floors crunch and prematurely aging the finishes. Tempura paint. Oil paint. Organic vegetable dyes. Once, just after Sabine's job offer, her boyfriend needed a pint of blood, but he was scared of needles so he made it from boiled beets.

"It's too purple," Sabine said, peering into their only large pot, roiling on the stove. Now and then a hunk of tuber would pop to the surface. "Maybe add turmeric? The yellow might balance it out?"

"Purple and yellow make gray," he said, and she could tell he was trying to keep his voice calm. "Any true artist would know that. I said it before, and now it's coming true. You are selling out."

"I'm not," Sabine said. "I just can't do the coffee thing anymore."

"You used to make the most beautiful bird-scapes," he said. He was wistful as he stirred the pot of desiccated beets. He threw in a handful of beet tops, a neutralizing green.

It was hard for her to describe to him why she'd quit the bird-scapes—her word, which she did not point out he was appropriating, for the canvasses she outlined nature scenes on and then filled in with feather. When she'd first started, in high school, the project had seemed very pure and she had spent hours collecting fallen feathers, but as time went on, it was easier to purchase in craft shops or online. After one spin through the washer at the laundromat, crammed into an old pillowcase and washed on hot, her bagged, store-bought feathers were ragged enough to pass for having been found on the forest floor.

And at first, she'd only used pine tar or other kinds of pitch and sap to affix the feathers to the hand-stretched canvas boards she'd cut herself with a manual saw, but as time went on, she wielded a hot glue gun against whatever hangable surface she could find on sale. There just wasn't time to do it all—work and school and scavenging. At the very beginning of her junior year, she'd landed a solo show, but the only piece that had sold was the worst of all of them—synthetic down pasted to a bed of rayon and glitter in a cheap attempt at *Starry Night*. She priced it at $4,567.89. The ascending numbers were meant to be a marker to anyone who actually cared about art, because she was embarrassed of the piece, but the enormous eighteen-by-twenty-foot canvas filled the space for the other works she didn't have. She was even more humiliated that someone wanted to buy it, and absolutely deflated when she cashed the check, even though it got her more than current on rent.

Still, her boyfriend had been impressed by her take, and he delighted in its irony.

Now that she had spent more time at a proper office, and more time with her coworkers, especially Michael who was the closest to her in age, she thought about it differently. *Consecutive pricing*, she could have called it, the string of ascending numbers. It could even be a way to bid. Start with five, and go from there. $543.10; $5,431; $54,310.

Her boyfriend didn't know Michael, but that didn't stop him from not liking him.

He would never say his name, only "that guy." *That guy you sit with, that guy you work with, that guy—wait, why are you having lunch with that guy?*

At the office, she and Michael didn't talk about art, though Sabine thought about it as she worked through her slides, through her tables. At first, she knew so little, she was constantly at the help files, and she hoped Raul and Penelope and Jane and Chrysa also had a nicely tabled instruction set detailing exactly how to proceed.

She'd heard Penelope and Raul had patched things up, and Chrysa was doing a series of observations:

Oh, it's so stable—
You at your screen. What about
The rest of your life?

Sometimes she looked up and Michael would be looking at her, and then he would look away, though Sabine would not. Once, after a long weekend, the elevator opened to the twelfth floor and Michael was just outside the door. He'd been in early, was headed out for coffee.

And there was a pull there, in the way he looked at her, the way he touched her shoulder.

"Oh, hi."

"Hi."

"Coffee?" he asked.

"I'm fine," she said, but she was not fine. The spot on her shoulder was burning. This was what her boyfriend Ryan/Sebastian had seen before she'd seen, the way she wanted to pull Michael to her. She wished she'd worn something different than her same rumpled twinset and black pants.

Then they were exchanging places, she stepping outside of the elevator and he stepping in, and then the doors were closing and he was whooshing through the building, past the debt collectors on floor ten, the solar engineers on six.

She imagined him descending, swiftly, away from her. She depressed the button on the elevator, to call the next car, but the elevator was taking forever, and she didn't know where, exactly, he might get coffee from; there were many places and among many other things she didn't know about Michael, she didn't know which shop was his favorite.

Sabine turned from the elevator bank and headed for the stairs. At eleven, she passed Melissa, earbuds in, slim thighs hiking the flights. At seven, a group of workers arguing. By the time she burst through the lobby and into the street of her downtown building, Michael was long gone. A light rain had started, and she spotted Kate, sheltered by a polka-dot umbrella, crossing the street. Even though at home Sabine and Sebastian/Ryan talked a lot about feelings, she didn't think she could explain this feeling to him, how all she'd really have to do was wait for Michael to come back, his latte steaming, but also how it seemed impossible to wait. How she liked Kate but didn't want to talk to her in this moment. How the way the condensation rising from the manhole covers and the cars splattered with just a few sparse rain drops seemed inexplicably and terminally sad. How the consultant who had helped her had texted her and asked how the new gig was going and wanted to know if he could take her to sushi, and how she had known exactly what the pretext was, but eating raw fish on cold rice and getting fucked in a loft sounded nicer than her boyfriend and his beets.

How, when she looked at the sidewalk, the concrete dark with dirt and damp, there was a single feather, and how, whether fallen from the sky or loosed from a scavenging pigeon's wing, as much as she wanted it, Sabine simply could not bend, would not pick it up.

THE CIRCLE

In my office, my coworkers complained about the HVAC; they complained about Kate, my boss, and they complained about the roaches that crept around the copy machine and slunk through the restrooms. I didn't like the roaches either, but the complaining, it just wore me out.

*

The entire summer when I was thirteen, I slept outside, sometimes at the foot of Barb-Ann's yurt while she stayed in my bedroom (that summer, she was in love with Pablo, but they needed space) and sometimes in the soft grass that had grown up around one of the converted school buses where a boy I liked lived with his parents. His name was Jay, short for JayBird, because as a child, he had squawked at everything.

*

The Circle, where I had grown up, had never been a planned commune.

A few wood-framed houses, some inherited land, and then a fire pit, a steam lodge, what became an outdoor kitchen, and then a ring of converted buses and vans, campers extended by tarps and wall tents, yurts, army surplus gear, four tipis, and the occasional bivy sack nestled between. Wood smoke and drums. Garden sheds filled with beef and marijuana, hanging to dry. The ticking of solar panels and the occasional roar of a generator. Carpets of pine needles, of gravel, of mud, of snow. Bare feet. Bee boxes and herb gardens. A spring-fed well. The outhouses off to the side, flanked by the collection of working and half-working rigs that belonged to anyone who could reach the pedals or was willing to take a chance on a roll-start. Either a push from behind, or pushing yourself (half in and half out of the cab), gripping the wheel while nudging the rickety truck down the incline, and as the speed picks up, just at the bottom, just where it's about time to pound the powerless brakes, jam the gear into first and pop the clutch and cross your fingers for the engine to engage. If it works, you'll lurch some, but hope is like that.

*

In the office, I always took the stairs, and I wore a set of white headphones connected to an old Walkman I had found at the Goodwill. I listened to tapes of birdcalls or studio sessions with Peter Tosh. I also liked Vivaldi and Cat Stevens, because both put me in a good mood.

*

In our home study, we'd learned that dreadlocks were not only worn by us, Circle people—a mostly white group in the Rocky Mountains— but also by ascetics, Islamic dervishes, and sadhu Hindis who have left behind all material attachments to live in caves and forests and temples.

It was a rite, and we could choose it at puberty, for girls on their first menses. I was eleven. We didn't think we were appropriating hair. We were Samson, we were Rasta, we were our own Nazarites.

*

I had hitchhiked to Denver. I had found a small studio apartment. I had purchased the first razor I had ever owned in my life and had shaved my body from toe to crown.

I was as smooth as shell, smooth as soap.

*

In Denver, I had been working in a natural foods store that hired me on the spot, based on my knowledge of essential oils alone. When I later talked to my mother about trying for an office job, I could hear her frowning. It had been hard to get her on the phone. There was only a single receiver in The Circle, and frequently the bill was unpaid.

"This is about money? Maybe you should get a roommate," she told me. "It's not natural to live alone. You don't see this in nature."

"Bears are solitary, Mom."

"Bears are an exception," she said.

"Moose are solitary too," I said.

"Well, Melissa, you aren't a moose or a bear. You are a human animal and humans are social. Get a roommate."

"I don't want a roommate."

"You can't make decisions about life based on money," she said.

"I changed my hair," I said.

"Oh Mel," she said. "Really, get a *roommate*."

"You sound well," I said.

"Thank you," she said. "I'm fine, but I miss you."

*

At first, I had tried to untangle my dreads. The natural foods store where I worked had a cream that was supposed to help loosen the hair, and I applied it and soaked my head in a bucket of hot water, like the directions said. Then, I started at the ends, trying to pick the strands loose, but mostly the hair broke off and ended up on my floor. After a week of this, I had only a few inches free and I was out of cream.

It was easier to shave than I had thought. First, I clipped close to my scalp with my kitchen scissors, and then it seemed so simple to take off what was left, razor sparkling. The shock turned out to be the slow kind, catching my reflection in a window, bald head wrapped in a scarf, or later, when there was a pinky's length of hair and it was curling. As a child, my hair had been perfectly straight.

I wondered what else I would find out about myself.

*

Once, when I had saved up a few vacation days, I hitchhiked home, on the summer solstice, and I slept again in the thick grass. My hair had grown just to my shoulders, and I wore it in a single thick twist secured as a reference to what I couldn't keep. In the mornings, my curls were tangled with twigs and green leaves.

My parents tried to talk me out of going back to Denver. My dad said a recent crop of mushrooms had just come in, very good, very potent.

"I have to work on Monday," I said. "I can't go into the forest just now."

They gave me a good send-off on the side of the highway as we waited, though. A drum circle started up and they danced, and I danced with them. There were a few horns, a single reed, Barb-Ann's clarinet, and their voices, which had been made strong by years of impromptu singing. After thirty minutes or so, the driver of the car who stopped for my outstretched thumb got gifts of chokecherry jam and carob cookies. It was an older woman, she said she knew of The Circle but had never lived there.

We rode the rest of the way in silence until the outskirts of the city began to show. She pulled into a gas station.

"I don't do door-to-door," she said. "You know where you are going?"

"Yes, I have an apartment," I said.

"Be careful," she said.

*

We did not participate in Western medicine. Instead of vaccines, my mother gave me Echinacea, colloidal silver, oil of oregano, and my father prepared poultices of mail-order and local herbs, bandaged onions to the bottom of my feet, dosed me with elderberry.

In mornings, when my father pulled the onion slices from my feet, wrapped in cheesecloth, we'd examine.

"See how it's changed color," he'd say, turning the slices over in his hands. "That's because it's drawing out the toxins that were in your body."

In my own kitchen, in my own city apartment, once I left a cut onion out overnight on the counter and woke to the same grayness. And ear candles too. After years of rolled-up newspaper dipped in beeswax, I burnt a retail ear candle from the natural foods store down to its nub while attached to nothing, and the results were the same—crud sucked up into the flue.

It's not that they were backwoods, my parents, or unintelligent. They had DDT kidneys; they grew up when doctors smoked cigarettes during surgery. I was born from them, and their idea of the world and what they wanted from it, and what they wanted was purity.

*

In the office, people were not doing well. Kate was going through a divorce, and Michael and Sabine were in some kind of desire loop that we'd never see in The Circle. In The Circle, they would have already screwed and would have gotten on with choosing each other or moving on. Instead, all of us stared at spreadsheets. I listened to cricket sounds and Jim Croce on my headphones. Kate reported a dead roach in the bathroom. Sabine said she was glad the roach was dead.

*

When I was twelve, our neighbor Claire came back from a visit to relatives in Kansas with chicken pox. It was a gift for us, a shot at natural immunity. There was a Pox Party, where we were all encouraged to lick from the lollipop—cinnamon and vanilla, homemade, perched on a barbeque skewer—that Claire had held in her mouth all morning.

I want to say I can remember my mother admiring the speckle of Claire's skin, but I'm not sure if that is true. Still, willowy and slight, blond to a degree of translucence, Claire had the potential to be a change agent.

Her cake, tiered and pink. We rarely got sugar, and so we tucked into the frosting with abandon. She had so many presents. I had given her a broach, or my idea of one, a flower I'd cut from felt and then secured three beads and glued it all to a safety pin. My mother helped find a box to place it in and helped me fold down the edges of an inside-out brown paper bag and tied it all with a green cloth ribbon.

After the party, we heard Claire's fever had spiked, the rash worsened, and finally, against the advice of The Circle, her parents took her to the hospital in Frisco.

I wouldn't know until years later, when I was researching, worried about my immunization status, that there were fewer than a hundred fatalities from chicken pox annually in the US. It is an airborne disease, so the lollipop could not have been that effective.

Claire did not leave the hospital and passed a few days later.

The scientific name for chicken pox is *Varicella*.

Almost a pretty word.

*

In Denver, the first time I called my parents—which meant dialing the only Circle house with a phone and then waiting for someone to find them—I gave them my address. Four days later, I came home to a battered box the post office had dropped at my door. Inside, jar after jar of homemade jam and pickled beans, venison jerky wrapped in a cloth, and a tin of the sourdough bread starter we'd always had at home, wrapped with a note from my mother. *Not sure if this will survive the trip. Give it a good sniff & test with a small batch. XOXO & One Love to you, Daughter.*

*

Once, when the business was not doing well and they put all of us on an involuntary furlough, I went home in winter. I didn't arrive until it was already late, and I thought my parents would have space for me, but the house was already holding too many. I could have found a place on the floor, but I hoisted my old pack and tromped through the snow and knocked on the school bus door, holding my sleeping bag.

Jay's parents had gone to Taos, permanently, for the sunshine, and the bus was his. He let me in. The place was clean and he had a propane cooktop and an herb garden growing under a full-spectrum bulb, and a pretty quilt covered his bed.

The hard work and clean food had made Jay's skin glow. Though I ate clean in my own way, I could not compare to the radiance of Jay.

"I remember you, Melissa," he said. This was the way he talked, the way they all talked. Always some kind of meaning.

"I remember you too, Jay," I said, because I had grown up with him and because I knew how to do this.

He was making tea, but the kettle had not yet started its scream. He offered me a joint and I took one small toke from it, just enough to smooth.

As the water came up to boil, he kneaded my shoulders—an old trope, but he was good at it and it felt good.

The cups were set out already. I poured the boiling water over the loose leaves.

"It's cold tonight," he said, and he led me toward the quilt, our mugs in hand.

Over a decade ago, in my sleeping bag, we'd only spooned—tightly, yes, two people in a one-person space—and we'd petted a bit. Mostly we kissed. We were children.

Jay put his tea down, took my tea and set it on the side table, and pulled my hips to his hips. He laced his fingers at the top of my jeans and undid the button and zipper so deftly I hardly noticed until he was undoing his own. He eased off my jeans, my flannel shirt, my undershirt, my bra. I wondered where he'd learned to unhook the clasp; brassieres were not popular among Circle women. He heaped his clothes on top of mine.

When I felt his sex on mine, there was a moment when I wondered why I had ever left. I was sure he could belong to me, if I chose him.

In the morning, when I woke, the fire from the woodstove had gone out. I was sticky and cold and Jay was snoring. I built a new fire and lit the propane burner for coffee, but all I found was matcha, so I steeped it in a cloth filter and brought it to Jay, steaming, and woke him.

"It's like heaven," he said.

"Good morning," I said. I already knew he'd be angry at me later. One night together didn't make a lifetime, but I knew in the way Jay gripped his mug, the way that he opened the quilt for me in an invitation to come back to bed, to stay, that he wanted me there, to stay with him, curled on his parents' old mattress and holding skin to skin, because that's how Circle people would think—what else is there to hold on to, besides one another.

*

Sometimes in the office people would be complaining about the temperature, or the burnt coffee, or the copy machine jamming, and I would think about my dreads. I wasn't ashamed of wanting a different life than what my parents had, but I missed the kindness.

There were a lot of things I'd had to learn to do—how to write a résumé, how to dress. How to plug in the headphones to keep the sounds of the office out. How to remind myself that I'd picked this.

*

When I'd first come to Denver, I'd done it with the money I'd made working three seasons for Ritchie in an old camp trailer, shaping big, dried marijuana buds into tidy, saleable nuggets. Everyone said if you could get fast at it, there were big operations in California where you could make a year's wage in a month. Even wearing gloves, I had a contact high that made the dim light and the heavy air of the trailer seem dreamy.

When I got to Denver after my first leaving of The Circle, I called Ritchie, from a pay phone. I had hitchhiked, seen the mountains bleed into the foothills and then flatten to abrupt plains. I was just on the edge of the city, but he sent a taxi for me.

At Ritchie's house, there was a large dog and an even larger stereo system. I did not ask the dog's name, and Ritchie did not tell me. The trailer I had once worked in was parked in the yard. He gave me whiskey in the early afternoon, and we talked in fragments between his phone ringing and people coming in, going out. Like the dog, there were no introductions.

By the time the sun was down, I was very drunk and very stoned and very tired, and I lay down on Ritchie's spare bed, and just as the room stopped lurching from a tilting spin, he was there, lifting my torso upright to give me a drink from a glass of ice water. The water felt like creek melt, quieting my stomach with cold.

I heard the dog bark. I opened my eyes all the way. The light on the side table was switched on, or perhaps I had never switched it off, and I saw that Ritchie was naked, the hair at his crotch a gray wire.

"Go back to sleep, Melissa," he said, relaxing the arm that was supporting me and then turning out of the room, his ass glowing in the lamplight.

I stayed awake for the rest of the night, eyes on the room's door, listening for the latch, listening for the dog. The moment the first sun broke through the bedroom window, I was up and on my way out, my camp pack hitched tightly against my back. I stepped over Ritchie, splayed on his living room rug. He had put on jeans, but no shirt, and his hair covered his face.

I walked for a long time, and I wondered what my parents would say. *Probably something about being uptight about nudity*, I thought. It felt good to walk, good to be in the morning air. I kept my eyes focused on the high-rises glinting in the distance.

*

I kept my apartment for a long time, even though corporate life suited me in a certain way and I could have afforded more. I saved. I moved up. I grew my hair, longer and longer, but kept wearing it in a single twist. I was starting to make very good money, not quite Ritchie money, but doing okay, but I didn't get a car. A car seemed extravagant.

*

Once I went home in spring, just as mountain foliage was waking up, and the air was clear and golden, and The Circle was starting to prep their gardens and replenish their chickens.

My mother was distraught because the cow had died, and age was making her less comfortable with the reality of farm life, the way mortality was everywhere. She had seen the glass of the old girl's eye turn cloudy, seen her fall in the field.

By this point, my hair was halfway down my back.

"I think Jay has a line on a calf," my mother said.

"How much would a cow cost," I said. "I could arrange it."

"We're so happy he's still here, Melissa," she said. "People are leaving. You left, and it opened something. More leave every year. We worked so hard."

*

A few weeks later, when I was fired, there were sixteen of us, sixteen crammed into the elevator while it groaned. It was the first time I'd been in it, always preferring the stairs. We were pressed hard against each other's bodies while trying to negotiate the boxes from our desks—and why, why did we think we even wanted these things, half-used pens and white-out, the mostly dead plants leaking dirt, the ragged notebooks full of meeting notes. A few of us might have had framed photos, worth keeping, but I did not. I had, in a handle bag from the lunch spot, a roll of packing tape because I was out at home, some .07 mm pencil lead because I was also out at home, and a pad of lime-green sticky notes because I liked the color. I was happy with the handle bag, slung on my wrist and hanging at my side, instead of a box pushing into my rib cage in the crush of newly unemployed bodies.

On the street, I dropped my bag and pulled my hair loose from the twist, the wind off the Front Range already blowing it into knots. I liked the ragged feel of it. In the west, there was still snow on the mountains and flurries speckling the foothills.

It would take a day or two to pack the apartment, and a fraction of a day to travel home. I used my cell phone to phone my mother, waiting while the wind whipped and someone's child ran to find her.

"Of course we have room," she said. "Oh, and Jay found a cow."

I remembered the drums, the fires, the grass, and the cold.

I remembered Claire.

Just for a little while, I thought. Figure a few things out.

The wind picked up and my bag blew into the street. I put my hand to my head and the tangling had already grown thicker. In a gust, a ragged leaf stuck, and then the thread of a plastic streamer like the kind from the handlebars of children's bicycles. As the wind became fiercer, my hair caught a scrap of silver paper, a small and smooth hunk of glass worn down from being on the pavement, and then yarn dropped from someone's knitting, and then a thin washer separated from its bolt, and by the time I had walked home, my tresses were heavy from debris and starting to bind.

Of course Jay found a cow, I thought, digging out the old camp pack and stuffing it with clothes. I packed a few kitchen things and some food into boxes pulled out of the recycling bin in the alley. I thought of the cow and how long it had been since I had touched a beast, pulling milk into a pail. My first dreads, for years, were stashed in a paper bag tucked above the refrigerator—I took those too.

I had some furniture, a few framed prints on the wall. I packed and I thought of the razor, how it had been so efficient, how it had shone.

Faster, I thought, *before you change your mind.*

I didn't need a sofa, I didn't need a toaster or a bathroom rug, so I hauled the handful of boxes and my pack to the corner. I would call my landlord in the morning, apologize.

On the street, the wind was still blowing, damp and urgent. Bark from someone's yard mulch and a dropped earring flew to my hair.

I was traveling heavier than when I'd left The Circle, but the weight didn't bother me. I thought it could be awhile before I got a ride, but I was prepared to leave the boxes if I had to. A truck or a hatchback would take some luck, but was not impossible.

I phoned my mother again.

"I may be there by tonight," I said.

"If you can get here by dinner, Barb-Ann is making an outrageous chili," she said. "I'll hold some back for you either way."

"I'll try," I said.

I went to the corner, and I put out my thumb.

THE CROW

On the night his sister came, Michael's mother was taken to the hospital in an ambulance. Even Michael, a boy of eleven, knew this was not the way it was supposed to work, but he wasn't sure what had gone wrong. His stepfather, Dave, followed in the car and told Michael to wait at home.

The pregnancy had come very quickly after his mother and Dave's wedding. Finally, after midnight, Dave called and had him take a taxi to the hospital. Michael liked Dave, who met him in front of the hospital, but he didn't love him, at least not in the same way he loved his mother.

Dave told him that things had stabilized, but still, there was his mother, in a state of intubation. He didn't learn this word until later, but the tube terrified him then, and later on sometimes he would wake from a dead sleep, thinking of it. He had learned that the tube—placed in the trachea to aid breathing—was supposed to be helpful for a patient's respiration, but all he could think of when he first saw his mother's mouth propped open by plastic, was how the tube must have pressed against her; he had wondered how she could possibly do anything without gagging. Later he would learn that patients who are intubated are also sedated.

And his sister. He could have fit her in the palm of his hand, if he was allowed to touch her. In the Neonatal Intensive Care Unit, which they would learn to call the NICU, she was also with a tube. They both had IVs, his mother and his sister, and in their respective rooms, the screens of the medical equipment mirrored and displayed what was happening in their bodies, and it terrified him, watching his mother's blood pressure tick up or tick down, his sister's heart rate racing and slowing.

Before his sister was even home, Dave wanted Michael to do counseling. His stepfather was very different from what Michael could remember of his biological father. His stepfather cried, his stepfather sometimes put his hand on the back of Michael's neck, his stepfather made homemade pesto in a food processor and rarely raised his voice. A vegan, his stepfather Dave didn't eat meat, or cheese, or even honey. He wouldn't wear leather. He worked in an office. Michael's biological father had rarely worked, and Michael wasn't sure if he could cook. He didn't know much about the guy, actually, and his mother never volunteered.

The counselor told Michael to practice breathing. He prescribed yoga and Pilates, and his stepfather checked out DVDs from the library and then made copies so they could watch them again and again, and he did the exercises with Michael. In the living room, they'd put on sweatpants and old T-shirts and count through the hundreds or lift into a downward-facing dog, breathing in, breathing out.

Michael wasn't sure if the exercises were really helping, but Dave said they couldn't hurt. Dave said he *could* feel his sacrum opening, just like the video instructor said, and together they looked up a picture of how that last heart-shaped bone in the spine fit together with the wings of the hips, and Dave read the unusual words out loud, *ilia* and *coccyx*, and the easier-to-pronounce but more embarrassing-sounding *pubic bone*.

When his sister came home from the hospital, two and a half months had passed. Michael wondered about the expense of it, but he didn't ask because he'd heard Dave tell his mother not to worry. His mother and his stepfather were very happy that baby Leah—she was still so small—was with them in the house. She wore oxygen strung under her nostrils and a fleece onesie. Michael had held her a few times in the hospital, later, when she was allowed to be out of her Isolette, but mostly he did not go to the hospital. His mother went to her office, and his stepfather to his, and after work they would meet at the NICU and check in on his sister while Michael let himself into the house and did his homework and his yoga.

By the time his sister was discharged, Michael could loop into a wheel—a full backbend, with palms and feet on the floor and the spine curved between them—and almost lift to crow. He had the arm strength to lift his back haunches off the floor and balance the top of his thighs on the back of his upper arms, but he could only hold it if he kept his head tipped down toward the floor, and if his gaze moved even a little, he would tumble. Dave had less time to practice with him, but he would join when he could, and Dave was impressed by the tentative crow. Now that his mother didn't have to go to the hospital every day after work, even she would join occasionally, if his sister was sleeping. He thought there was no way his mother could do the crow, but she learned it much more quickly than Michael had. The instructor on the video said *bakasana* was about balance more than strength. His mother could even, while in the pose, tap her toes together, and soon she was inching up higher and higher, into a half handstand.

When he saw the way she laced her ankles, he understood how the pose had gotten its name—she did, there with her arms bent into the triangle of a wing, and her body tucked up tightly, look something like a bird in flight, but he wondered about her breath, if she would be okay up high, where the air is thinner, or if maybe, cloaked in feather and in a hollow-boned body, the atmosphere wouldn't matter so much, and in air, surrounded by air, moving easily through air, she would be just fine. Maybe she would never need the tube again.

*

After the divorce from his father, his mother used to tell him not to open the door for anyone when he was home alone, and he agreed to this, even though for years no one ever came to the door of their duplex. She also told him not to tell anyone he was there by himself. Sometimes the neighbor, a young mother also on her own, would call over the fence to Michael and he would call back, *yes*, he was okay. The neighbor had a toddler.

When Dave starting coming around, Michael was annoyed. He barely knew Dave, but it seemed like he was there all of the time. The first time Dave showed up before his mother was home from work, Michael refused to let him in. He peered through the crack made by the chain lock.

"I'm not supposed to open it," he had said, even though he was pretty sure it would be okay to open the door to Dave.

"That's smart," Dave had said. "Hey, I'll just sit out on the steps. We can talk like this."

It was a hot day, and Michael noticed Dave was sweating. Michael thought he should offer him some water, and so he brought a small cup and passed it through the gap in the door made by the chain lock. He was able to just barely squeeze the plastic between the door and the frame. Only a little of the water spilled. Dave thanked him. The duplex did not have a porch or an awning, just four concrete steps.

After Dave drank the water, he went to the trunk of his car. Michael watched him rummaging, and then Dave came back to the steps with an umbrella held over his head.

"My hair's pretty thin," he said to Michael. "I burn easy up top." He laughed.

"Why are you here, anyway," Michael asked.

"I came over to see you, and to see your mother," Dave said.

"She's not here," Michael said.

"I got that, bud," Dave said. "But you know, I like both of you, so I'll just wait. And that's one of the great things about being a grown-up, is that you can go see people you like, and you can wait for as long as you want."

Michael considered this, and even though Dave sometimes felt like an interruption, he had to agree.

"My mom will be home soon and she can open the door for you."

"Hey, no worries," Dave said, and he adjusted the umbrella.

When his mother had finally arrived, she wasn't angry at Dave for being there and she wasn't angry at Michael for not letting him in.

"It's hot," she said. "Who wants a Popsicle?"

"Me," Michael and Dave had said in unison.

*

When his mother told him that Dave had asked her to marry him and that she had agreed, nearly a year had passed since the day on the porch, and Michael asked his mother if she thought marrying Dave was a good idea.

"I wouldn't have said *yes* if it was a bad idea," his mother had said.

"But what if Dad is coming back?" Michael had said. "Dad will not like this."

He wasn't sure what to do with the look on his mother's face, crumpled at first, and then turned smooth, like a tire being inflated.

"He didn't leave us, Mikey. We left him, and no, we aren't going back."

He understood this. He was in fifth grade, and his father had been gone for what seemed like a very long time. Some of the kids at his school had girlfriends and boyfriends, in the childlike way of just beginning to understand what crushes were about, and he heard this from them too. *He didn't break up with me, I broke up with him.* He understood there was power in it.

"Sometimes I used to worry about him coming home when Dave was here," he had said.

Another look that he couldn't quite decipher, and then the fierceness of his mother's pull, catching him in both arms.

"I didn't know," she had said, her voice muffled, her lips pressed to his hair.

*

Dave was older than his mother, but he did not have any children and he had never been married before. The wedding was in Dave's backyard. Michael's new grandparents and a handful of friends were there. He didn't have grandparents on his mother's side. There was a photograph of them, but they had been dead for almost as long as he had been alive. He couldn't help but feel Dave's parents liked him a little bit too much. Like him, Dave was an only child.

"We never thought we'd have a grandbaby!" Dave's mom kept saying while she squeezed him. She was an old lady, but she smelled all right anyway, like cut flowers and sugar.

It was summer again, but the lawn was shaded, and there were small circular tables draped in white set up in the grass. A van came with food. Michael was not sure he had ever seen food delivered and then served like this. It seemed sophisticated and convenient, and of course, vegan. There was also a bar set up under a tree—it was like a restaurant, except the check never came.

When his mother put him to bed, in the room that would become his when they'd move next week, she asked if he had had a good time.

"I ate too much," Michael said.

"Good," she said. "Sleep tight, sweetie."

She was still in her dress. It was the first time he had seen his mother in anything so fancy, with a pleated waist and draped fabric at the sleeves. Instead of white, it was a powder blue so faint he didn't even notice the color until she leaned over to kiss him.

*

On the day his sister graduated off oxygen, Michael felt a change in the house. Without the tanks, his mother and Dave were calmer. His sister could move more easily, with no hardware to negotiate. Suddenly, Leah was a crawler, scaling her high chair when her parents were not looking, but Michael was looking. He let her go. He crouched by her, though, waiting for a slip, pressing his foot against the base of the chair to ensure it would not topple.

He admired her confidence, which seemed to come naturally. He also admired Dave, because he felt that Dave would never leave his sister, which meant never leaving his mother, or him.

"You're lucky," Michael whispered to his sister. "So lucky."

*

After Michael graduated from college, Dave got Michael the job in the office. It was a favor that Dave had called in, and Michael wondered about his biological dad, for the first time in a very long time. His biological dad probably could have hooked him up with better pot and the occasional bag of mushrooms, but not a straight job. Not health insurance. Not a parking pass.

It was a strange way to measure, and Michael understood this. He had come back to the small house because he wasn't sure where else to go. He had studied business management and communications in college, and at the time he had thought it was practical, but he found himself without a passion, and in the few interviews he went on, when they asked *Where do you see yourself in five years*, he balked. He was terrified. He had no idea where he would be, and he was—he had always been—an unsophisticated liar, and it was something he had known about himself for a long time, so he didn't even try.

At first, he had thought he would stay with his roommates, but they scattered to an MBA, to a marriage, to a teaching fellowship in Azerbaijan.

His sister was ten, and she had taken his bedroom, so he went into her old room, which was really a closet off the furnace. When he thought about it, he was surprised his folks had put her in the room in the first place; it had been renovated long ago, but it was still damp and smelled like gas, and there was only one low window. He considered that maybe he had been the pickier child, even though he had no reason to be.

At his office job, he worked at spreadsheets mostly, related to revenue analysis.

There was a woman there, Sabine, who he sat next to and who he was interested in, but she lived with her boyfriend. As far as Michael could tell, the boyfriend sounded immature and pretentious, but considering that he had never met the guy, Michael acknowledged he himself might be the immature one.

He didn't want to admit it, but even though the job was boring and felt meaningless, Sabine motivated him. When his supervisor praised him, he hoped Sabine heard. When he had finished his work but still had hours to burn and turned to others in his department to ask if they were slammed and was there anything he could help with, he hoped Sabine noticed. Melissa, another woman in the office, with her hiker's legs and her wad of long curly hair, might have been considered prettier than Sabine, but he liked Sabine because she was an artist.

When he told Dave about her, his stepfather shook his head.

"The office is not your dating pool, Mikey," he said. "Be careful with that. It's fine when you are going out with someone, but then if you break up, you have to see them every day."

"I think I could handle that," Michael said.

"It's still not a good idea," Dave said. "I would advise you to tread very lightly."

"Where'd you meet Mom, again?" Michael asked.

"Okay, bud," David said. "Your mother worked in the building I used to work in. Of course, you already know that." Dave pulled a beer from the refrigerator, offered it to Michael, and popped the cap of one for himself.

"And? If you had broken up? You would have had to see her every day."

"That's where you are wrong about this Sabine thing," David said. "It's not the same. I talked to your mother every day for three years by the time she was splitting up with Ben."

Michael swallowed hard. No one ever said his father's name, and it registered quickly.

"I wasn't trying to save Clara; she was crying a lot, you know, right at her desk, but everyone understood. It was hard for her. She worried about you. When she finally left him, I think the whole building was relieved. I don't think I was the first person to ask her out."

"So, you think I should wait for Sabine to break up with her boyfriend?"

Dave took a long drink of his beer. "I think you should be okay with Sabine doing whatever Sabine wants to do. I think if Sabine has room in her life for you, then it will work out, and if she doesn't, it won't, and you need to be okay with it either way."

In college, Michael had had one single relationship, with a very shy girl who had a magnificent collection of candles. In her small studio, she had a metal table that held the display—tiers of discards from bottles of wine and liquor, perfume or cordials, made from vintage glass and new, knitted together with wax. There were a few proper candle holders, but any container was scrubbed or picked clean of labels, because she said the reflection was better. She had laid a fire blanket beneath the table, just in case.

At first Michael thought it was an altar, but she said it was not.

"How do you move it?" he had asked.

"I break it apart, and then in a new place, I fill in the holes with new bottles and new candles until it's fused again," she had said.

In some areas, she had pressed mismatched earrings and rhinestones and small figures into the wax. When they had sex, on her mattress, which was near the candles, the fire light blazed on them, but he understood her not-altar was the most important thing in her life.

He did not know what the most important thing in his life was.

*

Michael wasn't always sure how to interact with his sister. She went to school, she did her homework. No longer a very small girl, she was just a bit smaller than average. She wore glasses at a young age, but Dave also wore glasses at a young age, so this was not to be remarked upon. What Michael hadn't expected was his sister's reverence for him. When he came home from work, she begged him to help her with her homework, and he did. One day, he showed her how to plot out the calculations for her math programs in Excel, and she brought the crisply printed spreadsheet with her to school, but her teacher was not impressed.

"She said it was cheating," his sister said.

"It's not cheating," Michael said.

"That's what she said," his sister said, "and she's the boss."

"I still want to help you," Michael said.

Leah. He called her Lee. It was hard for him not to remember her as she had been when she first came to them, just a speck of a child, the tubes under her nose and the tube in his mother's throat, some different, plastic birth cord.

Now she glowed. She glowed yellow like his ex-girlfriend's candles, she glowed blue like his mother at the backyard wedding in her powder dress, she glowed red like Dave's face the first day he came to the door.

"Get your pencils," Michael said, and she ran for her backpack.

Waiting for her, he remembered what life was like in the beginning with his mother and Dave, and then after Lee was born. How when she was on the respirator, he was working on the crow. How he didn't understand until now that it was his prayer to her, his clumsy attempt at yogic flight.

It had been years since he had been practicing his therapist's yoga, but he felt the urge then, to bend into *bakasana*—could that be the right word, he wondered, but he felt almost sure it was—to lift his feet from the floor, and to balance his weight on his fingers.

He went to the floor. After such a long time, he was not sure if he could do it, and his sister had returned, her open school bag leaving a trail of papers. From a squat, he splayed his palms on the linoleum and start to lean the weight of his body forward, hooking his knees behind his elbows.

"What is that?" Leah asked, and he did his best to explain to her what the posture meant. He remembered the calm voice of the instructor's voice on the library videos.

"Try it with me," he said.

She joined him, and there was a second, tipping, where he thought they both might fall. As he shifted his full weight onto his arms, he lifted his toes from the ground, and his sister rose beside him. She was so light and had so much youth on her side, flight was easy.

CHRISTIAN

NOT US

It wasn't until my second wedding that my first divorce really sank in. I was under the gazebo, waiting for my bride, Raquel. Raquel with the long auburn hair, tips dipped green, pink feathers woven in, and a braid with a purple ribbon wound around the crown of her head. Raquel, white dress, stitched with rhinestones and fake pearls. Raquel, whose borrowed diamonds from some rich friend made my ring to her look like a speck of mica. Raquel, barefoot on the grass that led up to the gazebo.

We wrote our own vows. We had the most perfect, meringue-light cake, spun sugar decorating it with such a halo it seemed a pity to cut—the wisps and the frosting cleaved under the ceremonial knife, the marzipan and fondant crumbled. We smiled. We didn't jab the cake into one another's faces, we only touched a bit of buttercream to each nose.

Then, endless bottles of golden champagne. It had only been an hour or so, but we were already remembering our parents in the front row of the padded folding chairs, who looked like silver and burnished pewter instead of their usual plain gray.

Raquel, in the aisle, coming toward me.

Raquel, lit perfectly in the afternoon light.

I had met her at a party thrown at our house by my first wife, Rachel. The similarity in their names was just a coincidence. Rachel had been the administrative assistant at my job, and I was, and still am, the IT guy. One day when I was fixing her laptop, Rachel leaned in close to see what I was doing, and I leaned back. Sometimes it's that easy.

Rachel and I had gotten married one afternoon at the courthouse a building over from our office. Almost the entire staff had attended our wedding, and it was the kind of thing that people look back on and say they love about a job—when there is care and companionship in the day instead of just spreadsheets. It had been great fun, in that three-martini lunch kind of way.

Not even a year later, the night of the party, I met Raquel and learned she was an artist, a musician, a seeker. Raquel did not work at the company; she was merely a guest, the second cousin of our CFO. Our CFO's wife was busy, so she brought Raquel instead. Raquel told me about the collection of stones she'd gathered from different seas—the Black Sea, the Mediterranean Sea, the Sea of Cortez.

Only seas. Oceans, she said, were too big. Too awesome for one person to hold any piece of. Seas, she said, you could know. My wife, Rachel, didn't even have a passport.

I was in love immediately, and it was extremely awkward. Rachel and I had not even celebrated our first wedding anniversary, and I was obviously living in our shared home. Still, something inside of me had turned away from her, toward Raquel. It was like waking from a dream. Or falling into one. For example, I hadn't known that I longed to travel, and here Raquel had uncovered a desperate pull. I wasn't sure if she felt the same way, but within a week she had contacted me, and we made plans to meet up in Taos. To get away I'd had to weave a very elaborate story about my cousin in Santa Fe—how his laptop needed to be fixed, that he'd gotten it infected doing something personal and, since the machine belonged to the labs at Los Alamos, where he worked, he could get into career-limiting trouble. This much was at least true; my cousin did work at the Los Alamos labs, and if he did pick up a porn virus on his work machine, the Department of Energy would likely be extremely unhappy. But I hadn't talked to my cousin in probably two years, even though Santa Fe was not far from Denver.

"I'll come with you," Rachel had said. "It would be nice to take a little vacation."

"He's too embarrassed," I said. "And I want to respect that he trusts me to do this. It's kind of a confidential situation."

"Well, you just told me about it, so you can't think it's too confidential," Rachel said.

I agreed with her, but was still able to convince her not to come.

Raquel and I had decided to travel separately to make our first private meeting feel more like a rendezvous than a road trip. At a rest stop, I texted my cousin and asked him how things were going, how was work at the labs—establishing my alibi, I guess, in case I needed to.

Got a new job a while back, but things are good! You?

I texted him back, *Great! Things are going well!* And I said a prayer that my wife would not get curious and look my cousin up on LinkedIn.

As I drove from Denver toward the Colorado-New Mexico border, I did have a moment where I wondered just exactly what I thought I was doing. When I saw Raquel waiting for me at the tiny adobe cabin we had rented, I felt sure that whatever I was doing, it was right.

It certainly felt right, two glorious days in the desert with my phone on silent and coffee under the pergola.

Rachel quit the office when I ended our marriage, and the same day she left, someone changed my picture on the intranet to a very unflattering snapshot from a company picnic instead of my ordinary headshot. And I should have been able to change it back because I had administrative rights to the server, but I could not. So, I knew this came from very high up—perhaps Dave, our COO, though he never struck me as the vindictive type. I sent malware to his computer anyway, and he lost two weeks' worth of work. Still, the photo remained. Remains.

Though I invited them all, almost no one from the office came to Raquel's and my wedding. Our CFO and her wife came, but they were family. I wasn't sure if it was timing or misplaced loyalty, but finally I decided I couldn't care about either. A bride, some friends, the fairy-land cake—I was surprised how much I loved all the traditional trappings—I didn't need the other people in the office, like Michael, or Sabine, or Kate, or any of them.

*

Maybe I was feeling a bit superior on our long-haul flight as Raquel and I made our way to our honeymoon at thirty-thousand feet, but I imagined that my ex-wife would think visiting the UK sounded very expensive and cold. My passport was about to get its first stamp. Raquel and I were headed to the Celtic Sea, first England and then on to Wales. After we landed, we spent our initial night in a noisy hotel room near the Gatwick airport. My joints were swollen from the long plane ride and made worse by a salty meal in the lobby that I'd eaten only because I was too tired to think about how it tasted and too hungry to care. My new bride snored beside me, but I was still buzzing from the travel and disjointed in time. We'd lost hours over the Atlantic. It wasn't something I was used to, though now I understood why Raquel had forced herself to stay up, even though she was dragging through customs, and she had barely kept her eyes open through our awful dinner.

Jet lag insomnia and the hard hotel bed—I wished Raquel had told me that she was working on a strategy to be able to sleep. All I saw was her on the brink of collapse, sober, but using the one-eye technique as we waited for our chips. Now she was snoozing, and I was wired awake.

It would be late afternoon in America, and I texted Rachel. This was not something I did often, but it was something I had started a few months ago. First, *Where are you working now? Just curious. I hope you like it.* And then, *I am sorry for how all that went down. Do you still talk to anyone from the office?* And the first one she replied to, *I'm selling the house, and since you paid half the mortgage for that year, my guy is going to contact you, and you'll get a check for your part of the pro-rated equity.*

Okay, Rachel had said.

After that, I'd occasionally send her an update about the house, or check in about something. Her answers were always quick and cheerful. A *Hey thanks for the $!* when the profit for the house was sent.

I'm in London, I tapped, thinking about the expanse of water between us. I wasn't sure if she would be impressed, and I wasn't sure if she would ask why I was there.

Fun, she wrote.

The cursor blinked on the little screen, and I wondered what the charges were for international communication.

It's wonderful, so far, I wrote.

Good!

I wondered if she had heard through the grapevine that I'd married. I figured she must have. *And also cold,* I tapped. *And really, really expensive.*

*

Long before Raquel, things at work had been weird for a while. Frankly, Rachel had seemed like she was the sanest of any of the women in the office. And I was trying to date again. When I'd first gotten the job, I was engaged, but in the first few months of my then-new job, the engagement had ended. That makes it sound like I was always trying to marry myself off. Maybe I was. I liked the idea. I liked the security of it. I liked the idea that I could be with someone and she would take my name and we could get old together, as one. My ex-fiancée, I will say, was not into the name-taking thing, and we fought about this. It was not until Rachel that I understood that I had been stupid to push my first serious ex.

Rachel also refused to take my name, though she was nice about it. When I told her I accepted it, she snorted and said there was nothing for me to accept. So, I learned that. I didn't even bring it up to Raquel. I could see the point about what a hassle the whole thing would be, especially now that I had a passport. But, love. Love is a hassle too.

*

In the morning, I woke to Raquel nuzzling me. I'd been dozing for a few hours at most, but she was rested.

"Let's consummate our marriage," she said, reaching for me.

"We did!"

"We haven't in Europe," she said, and this was hard to argue with.

Afterwards we showered and had coffee. We had breakfast at the hotel, and I actually quite enjoyed it. I called it *continental*, but Raquel reminded me we were not on the European continent. Then I scrolled my texts. Nothing, including nothing from Rachel.

We gathered up our things and left the hotel. Even though we were both in our early forties, Raquel had been determined to travel younger, so we had only backpacks. She didn't put it that way, "younger." She said, "Let's travel light."

Our packs were both blue, mine a bit less burnished. Raquel's hung against her spine like a child might, comfortable and slouchy, whereas mine was more like an adolescent grown too big for his skin and straining.

At our wedding, we had danced and danced and danced, and I'd finally kicked off my shoes to match her bare feet. The raised floor had been assembled just on the other side of our matrimonial gazebo. It was hard and equally as slick and sticky with spilled champagne and globs of cake, threads of sugar and bits of gravy from the buffet. There was also some danger there, we the only two with exposed soles, and our guests strapped into hard insoles and punishing heels—I watched my toes. Eventually some more of the women stepped into their stocking feet, but I was still looking out.

Swirl of dresses and shimmer and could I really believe this woman took vows with me—

"Hey, Christian—"

Raquel was passing a joint to me, and the minute I hit it, I was so grateful for no shoes and the way the floor felt under my feet, even the stickiness, even the threat of broken glass, even how my arches felt sore and tenuous. I was in a bubble, a beautiful, gauzy bubble. The music was slow, people were slow, my movement was slowing. And then one of Raquel's friends, well, one of my friends now, landed her spiked heel between my big and second toe.

At the reception, I had just winced and kept dancing though it really, really hurt, and I also didn't complain about the way the interspace between my first and second metatarsal throbbed on the plane ride. Not that I was going to admit to Raquel that I had had to look up foot anatomy on WebMD to get the language right, *if* I was going to complain, and *if* she had asked me about it.

*

"I wonder if I could take a few things out of this pack," I said, as we checked out of the hotel and went in search of a bus that would take us to the tube. I was remembering to call it the *tube*, not the *train*. Not the *subway*. "Maybe I could just ship some shirts or that other pair of jeans back."

"You're just thinking of this now?" A bus came by, but she waved it on.

It was raining. The hotel bill had been a bit more than I was expecting. "I hadn't noticed how stuffed it was until now that we are walking around."

Another bus came, and she pinched her eyes. She stepped back from the curb. "Not us," she said.

"I feel silly," I said.

Raquel nodded.

Once we got to central London, I hated the pack even more. In addition to its being overstuffed, I hadn't worn a backpack since college, and I handled it badly. Every five minutes or so, after I'd bonked them, some Londoner asked me to *please mind your bag*. Finally, we were in Trafalgar Square, just after lunch, sitting at a sopping table. I opened the pack and pulled out my rain jacket—which I should have been wearing—and a few changes of shorts, two shirts, and a pair of jeans and dumped them there on the pavement, feeling like a stupid, one-passport-stamp, bloated American.

"Better?" Raquel asked, as we walked to catch a train to our next hotel.

"I thought we were going to the Celtic Sea," I said.

"We're here, honey. It's all around us. Can't you feel it?"

I stopped my eye-roll just in time, before she turned.

*

I'm not going to say that I was perfect. I'm not going to say that Raquel was perfect. It's never like one person does everything right and the other person does everything wrong.

What I will say: on day four of our marriage, day five if there are some generous time change calculations, Raquel and I were in a stuffy bed and breakfast, and I was sleeping on the floor, searching on my phone—data charges be damned—for a return ticket home. Even though the weather was sleet outside, I was not cold. Suffocating, perhaps, but not cold.

"Jesus, Christian, get a grip," Raquel said, throwing a pillow my way.

"Gripping tightly, love," I said in my best British accent, which was awful.

"What are we fighting about again?" she asked.

"Just a lovers' quarrel, no matter!" This time, I thought the vowels were better.

"You sound like an idiot."

"Carry on!"

I heard her roll over in the bed. Something had happened on the train after I'd left my clothes in the square, and then something had happened as we'd checked into the small B and B on the coast. I had mentioned the weather. I said something about how I didn't know it would be so dreary.

"Missing your rain jacket?" Raquel had asked.

I got very angry then, because she was so smug. She could have told me way back in Denver that my pack was overstuffed. Maybe I didn't have passport stamps, but I had traveled domestically. I traveled with a proper—proper!—carry-on that rolled.

"Is this what you wanted, vagabonding in Europe?" I asked, as the man at the front counter returned our passports.

"Is this what you call 'vagabonding'?" she asked. "We have places to go. We have an itinerary. Jesus, we have credit cards."

Just one tip of her multicolored hair had faded, but in a pretty way, a stripe of pearl across her shoulder. Almost the same color as spun sugar.

Our room at the B and B was charming, if I had been in the mood for it. Otherwise, the bed was very small, which is how I ended up on the floor.

"It's not 'small,'" Raquel said. "It's European. Not everyone needs a California king just to sleep. Americans have beds the size of a small apartment. It's so wasteful."

"I think you are exaggerating," I said.

"I think you have no idea," she said.

*

In the morning, we got up early and had a short bus ride to Exeter, where we were planning on staying for a few days. Raquel wanted to go to Lizard Point, the southernmost tip of England. It would be another four hours via bus and train, and I was tired of traveling on public transportation. It was destroying my American sensibilities, I said, and Raquel said she would hire a car, but we couldn't afford it—even though we could afford it if we had wanted to.

"It's four more hours," I said. "Half a workday there, and half a workday back."

"Where's your sense of adventure?" Raquel asked.

"I'm tired," I said. "I think I have jet lag."

She'd washed her hair that morning, and even more of the color had come out. The green tips were more like a watery chartreuse.

Raquel was tired too; I could see it. "Like a fine Scotch moss," I said, fingering the ends of her locks, trying my accent again.

"Or a damn bad dye job. I'm kind of pissed about it," she said.

We decided we'd try for Lizard Point in the morning. We'd checked into a new B and B with a new tiny bed and the same old cloying air that everywhere had from keeping the windows jammed shut against the damp.

Then we spent the day darting between little pubs, drinking just enough to keep the edge off, but not enough to start talking. I'd given up on trying out my British accent, and Raquel had given up asking me if I was still mad "for no reason," as she put it. I tried to believe that it was only rain that we kept wiping from under our eyes.

That night, we were still tense, but I crawled into the small bed with her. I wondered how long we could really stay married if it was already going so badly, and then I wished I hadn't sold my house. Just as I put my head on the pillow, my phone lit up, and I saw Rachel's name.

I read the text but didn't reply. I moved to fit my body around my wife's in the way people who have a new love do, angling to touch as much of the other's body as possible.

"I'm sorry," I said.

"For what?" she said.

I understood that Raquel had an idea of what I should say, but I didn't know what it was. "All of it," I said, and hoped it didn't come out like a question.

Two puzzle pieces, mated, but just at the beginning. We were clenching tight, with no idea what the bigger picture would be. In the damp room. In the small bed. Our skin had started to gel together, cool and warm at the same time.

"I don't want to fight with you," I said.

"I know," she said, and then she slipped out of the bed, dragging a pillow along with her, and curled up on the floor.

TORNADO WATCH

In our home there were sounds. One of the sounds was like a balloon slowly deflating, a sound of almost nothing, of air being displaced, and I am not sure if we knew it was the canary in the coal mine of our marriage, which we were not paying very much attention to. So, we did not worry about it in particular, we only complained about the unplaceable noise. We checked the fridge and all of the other major appliances, we checked the HVAC system, we poked around outside the house and found nothing, but we kept hearing the slow, gentle whooshing punctuated occasionally by a squeak. Or the call of a suffocating bird.

We are paying the mortgage, and so I think we have some right to get whatever this is fixed, Jimmy, my husband, and I said to one another. We fiddled with the thermostat and took a flashlight to the crawlspace, and we called our insurance company, who kept wanting to know if we were opening a claim and we kept saying that we weren't sure, we weren't sure what was wrong—we were just trying to understand if we were covered.

We didn't know why it was so complicated.

We were married to one another, and we were also married to work, and we were married to our ideas, our ridiculous ideas—so caught up in the way laundry was folded or aspirational grocery lists. Most nights the produce rotted as we hit the booze. If we were drunk enough, we didn't hear anything, until finally that balloon must have released the final wheeze all at once, sputtering around like a firecracker through our house.

COULD YOU PLEASE, I'd written with Sharpie on a bright-lime sticky on a Tuesday before I left for work—the last day Jimmy slept in our bed—CALL A PLUMBER BECAUSE IT MIGHT BE THE PLUMBING? I didn't know it was the last day then. I didn't know until I came home and his own note was pasted on the countertop.

went to my moms

It wasn't like him to leave a note. Usually he texted.

We had met, Jimmy and I, just over a decade ago. We were both working in an office, and he was a contract employee, and when his contract ended, he asked me out. It was surprising. We had barely spoken; he was on a different team. We went on two dates, and the balloon filled up so quickly I thought it would pop. It was like a sharp intake of helium sucking the oxygen out of our bodies, like we already loved one another so much we couldn't breathe and we were only gasping hearts and guts. We were giddy and high and operating on an upper frequency.

We married on our fifth date—we made an impulsive drive to Blackhawk, Colorado, a casino town in the upper foothills of the Rockies. We both wore jeans, which was what we'd been wearing when we decided to get in Jimmy's car and go. Afterward, we rented a room at a hotel and then lay on the bed naked and wondered just exactly what we'd done.

We decided to sell our respective townhouses and get a place together. We decided we'd really make a go of it. We knew we were being reckless, but we didn't care. The first year of our marriage was in fact highly administrative, working backward through everything we hadn't done, like announcing our nuptials and getting to know one another in the day-to-day.

What we couldn't explain to people was how much grace our hasty commitment had given us. I wondered if this was what it was like in arranged marriages—we were already hitched, so we didn't have the luxury of enumerating deal-breakers because the deal was already done. In our first year, especially, we had to practice acceptance, constant continuous acceptance.

We thought it was a good foundation. At least I did.

And really, for how little we knew when we began, we took a long time to let out that last breath, for the balloon to finally deflate.

The night of Jimmy's note, our life had changed enough that I wasn't sure I wanted to fight for him, so I didn't call or text or email. I ordered a pizza and cracked a bottle of wine. I was sure he was not actually at his mom's, and I realized it was certainly not about the plumbing.

On our first date, I'd gone back to his place and we'd had sex on top of his messy bed and he kept saying to me, *Open your eyes*, and I did. He was inside of me and we kept our gazes locked.

*

I'm not sure if it was worse to sign the separation papers, or if it was worse to sign the severance papers at my job. We hide from our marriages inside of work, or we hide from our work inside of our marriages, and then when both are gone, it's like those dreams we had in elementary school, naked on the playground.

Naked on the playground would have been better—at least in those dreams, we aren't thinking about sagging breasts or a failing ass or getting foreclosed on. In those dreams, it's only children, sure, cruel in their moments, but it's not the same cruelty that comes with the full exposure of adulthood.

The last day at the office, after Dave, our COO, let me go, I went into the supply closet to get a box for my things and he followed me in. I'd been sweating at my desk while I collected my thoughts, but the closet was arctic. Reams of white paper like glaciers, piles of sticky notes like tundra flowers in bloom, a case of AA batteries ready to light up as bright as the aurora borealis, and the foot of an easel sticking out like a narwhal's horn.

"It's not easy for any of us, Kate," Dave said. "I had to fire Michael. Worst day of my career." Michael was his stepson.

"Michael stole our lunches," I said. All of the boxes in the supply closet were either too big or too small. "Yes, I am telling you, your kid was the lunch thief. I caught him once. You probably didn't know." Actually, I hadn't caught him. Heather had, and Heather had told me.

"He was? That's not why he was let go. It's revenue. It's the markets. We can't control the markets, though I wish I could," said Dave.

I was freezing, and I wondered if I really wanted anything in my desk, and I wondered why Dave thought I cared about the worst day of his career. I had always liked Michael. I had hired him, and I hadn't said anything about the lunches because I figured if that was his definition of rebellious bad behavior, he was probably fine. It occurred to me Dave did the firings because Dave was secure.

I abandoned the search for the box. "I think I'm going to just go home," I said. "There's nothing personal in my desk or on my laptop."

"I can be a reference for you," Dave said, shivering too.

"No, thanks," I said.

*

My job search was going okay. I wasn't working that hard on it. I had a little money from the severance, and I had a little money from the divorce settlement. The settlement money I didn't really want, and I hadn't asked for it, but I took it anyway. It was a surprise and I wanted to be open to surprises, even though the realization that my now ex-husband Jimmy had a large savings account he had hid from me stung. We weren't hurting financially and I wasn't a big spender anyway, so it was hard to believe his secret account had been anything other than a kind of a go-bag.

After we sold the house, I had a new apartment. I liked my place. It was small and compact, and it was mine. I bought bright fuchsia towels, because I could. I hung up my art prints, and rearranged my furniture, a mix of IKEA and vintage. Jimmy had always said my furniture was like a college kid's: cheap stuff paired with hand-me-downs from a grandma. He liked things to match. He had said we were professionals and we should have a more professional-looking home. I said he was welcome to redecorate any time he felt like it.

After the first rush of nestling into my new space and shopping, I neglected the laundry, and I ate ice cream for dinner.

I know. Ice cream for dinner is a single-lady divorcée cliché. Well, it's a lot better than making something in the microwave.

It was hard to shake the job, and it was hard to shake the divorce. It wasn't that I missed Jimmy or my work so much, it was that I had spent so much time in the swirl of the marriage crumbling and the swirl of the office with the weird wind in it, right in the center, where the hot half and the cold half came together. The physical office was just a suite badly in need of air-balancing, but now that I was at home all the time, I kept thinking about how every day when I'd walk in, I would flash on how tornadoes are made, the convergence of warm and cool air. I knew logically, at least after I looked it up, that a tornado has to be anchored to the ground and tethered to a cloud to really form, to do its damage with windspeed and lightning and hail and gravel flinging everywhere—I knew this was not happening in my office, but still! People get so casual, they get comfortable, and they overlook danger. They think it won't happen to them.

My friends asked me if I knew Jimmy was going to file, and I said, *Oh, yeah. Long time coming. Beat me to it.*

But I had no idea. And actually, he didn't just file, he had me served. After the note on the kitchen counter, it took only another three days for a courier to show. I knew something was up, re: *went to my moms*, but I didn't expect that. We'd always been nicer than that.

So, just like a tornado. Out of nowhere. I'm the cloud and he's the dirt. I overlooked the danger, too. Once it's going, watch out. I think I thought I was on the outside, or that I didn't understand what was forming. I thought we were tracking down a wheezing balloon, but really, I was in the middle of a storm and hadn't noticed. The eye, they call it. It's characterized by light winds and clear skies.

The whooshing sound we had heard, those winds. An exhale of atmospheric gas. It seemed like Jimmy must have known all along.

Open your eyes.

Also, with ice cream, it's the fancy flavors that get popular, like cookie dough or pints referencing jam bands. I like regular vanilla or chocolate. Strawberry is okay. I can handle a chunk of something mixed in on occasion, if I'm feeling adventurous, but generally I like my ice cream simple. I like my ice cream to reflect my vision for my life.

If there was ever a tornado flavor, I wouldn't try it.

*

After I was let go, I didn't see anyone from the office on purpose, not that anyone tried to see me. I had survived the first round of layoffs, the fiscally necessary ones, like when Dave fired his stepson/lunch thief Michael, and I had thought I was okay after that. Revenues recovered a little, and it seemed pretty smooth. I knew a couple of people from my team were riding out their unemployment and I thought I might be able to hire them back. Ideas of rebuilding felt good.

When Dave gave me the notice, it was just like getting served the divorce papers. Breezy, transparent skies collapsing into gray. Paper seems so harmless. Then when you lick an envelope, it cuts your tongue.

I wondered if no one from the office contacted me because I had been on edge for a while. Maybe they had come to dislike me. They all knew my marriage was falling apart, maybe they knew before I did, and also like a lot of people when their marriage is falling apart, I was drinking way too much, way too consistently. There was a feeling I had, and I am sure Jimmy had too, of waking up in the morning, sort of sliding open one eye, and just as the light hit, simultaneously praying there was coffee in the house but also hooch for when we got off work.

It's not a feeling we would have wanted other people to understand, planning around cocktails. The same way people plan their living room around their TVs.

At the office, I drank a lot of water. A gallon a day. I measured it in a quart jar, filled and consumed four times. *It'll change your life*, I would say to people in our cubicles. What I really meant was that perpetual hydration was the best bet against a hangover and maybe the only thing that was keeping me even remotely tethered to professional success. It kept the day-old alcohol smell off; it gave me something to reach for through the slog of conference calls and meetings. It was a sense of an accomplishment, when I'd hit that one hundred and twenty-eighth ounce. Like I'd done at least one good thing.

Even though I didn't really want to look for a new job, I was looking anyway. The ice cream had mostly replaced the alcohol, and I kept up with the water-drinking.

I took a sip of ice water; I took a spoon of vanilla. I rolled a cube around in my mouth, I took a spoon of pistachio—pistachio is another basic flavor. Overlooked, really, in the ice cream canon.

My teeth were cold.

I emailed a recruiter. I updated my profile on LinkedIn. Took a sip of water, took a spoonful.

Jimmy and I, we had barely spoken. The early years of our marriage, if nothing else, had taught me that I couldn't change his mind if it was made up, and they had also taught me that I didn't care to try, and not just with my husband. I think if my heart had turned in what seemed such a sudden way, he would have accepted it too.

went to my moms

Maybe he had, for a night.

In my old office, with the unpredictable temperatures, it was the cold that seemed to frustrate people the most. When it was hot, we all moaned and fanned ourselves, and the women cracked jokes about being of a certain age to never ask if a room was too hot, but the cold made people angry, bitter.

Now I felt a kind of attentiveness. I had read online about humans being highly adaptive to chilly temperatures, and I had heard a story on the radio about a man who ran marathon distances in very cold places with not much gear. The story had opened with him crossing a Colorado mountain pass in a car in disrepair, and having to blast cold air to keep the windows from fogging up. How in this moment he changed his mind to believe temperature was yet another construct. How there was no other way to get through it.

When I opened my living room window, the November air came in gently. More cool than cold, but still refreshing.

In the kitchen, I opened another window, put the ice cream back in the freezer, and took a handful of ice for my water.

I wondered what my ex-coworkers would think of me now, or what my ex-husband would think. I wondered what they had thought of me then.

I read somewhere that people who chew ice are sexually frustrated. I tried not to chew the ice, because I had also read that was very bad for your teeth.

I read somewhere about people going on ice cream diets and ice cream cleanses. This seemed ridiculous, but I was neither experiencing the massive stomach pains or weight gain/weight loss that others had reported on the Internet.

I read somewhere that people who have lost a job should keep a daily routine.

I read somewhere that people who get divorced should try new hobbies.

I read somewhere that people who have a high tolerance for cold simply perceive temperature differently, resetting their expectations of what comfort is either through training or necessity.

I didn't have a philosophy. I just liked the way the ice cream and the ice water felt going down, how I could feel a cool slide all the way to my stomach. I liked the edge on the late autumn air.

The trick, I realized, to avoiding disruptions like tornadoes or hydrogen fires, was to keep it consistent and not allow the possibility of convergence.

*

When Jimmy did finally reach out to me, it was another note. He'd put it in the mail. I was sure I had never seen him post anything, so the short letter felt like it had weight, coming from him. He'd had to write it, fold it, address it, stamp it. I read the single page three times. Mostly what it said was that he was sorry. But he didn't say for what, and he didn't say why.

We had given it quite a go, I thought, as I tacked the letter to my fridge. We had tried. I refused to believe a decade together was a failure. His did not offer an opinion, just the *sorry* in his sign-off, inked in his messy hand.

It was December by then, and the winter was bearing down. I opened a window to feel the bite of the cold as I read the letter for the fourth time.

The ink was different, but I saw:

went to my moms

The room felt out of oxygen.

Open your eyes.

I closed the window.

COULD YOU PLEASE CALL A PLUMBER

I poured a glass of water and dropped some cubes in.

Melissa, Michael, Tabatha, Mariette, Brian, Julie, Christian, Laird, Jorge, Dwayne, D'Shawn, Sabine, Trung, Roger, and Sommer—the group I had worked with from the office. We'd been let go separately, but I felt like I had a memory of riding the elevator down to the ground floor with them, the sixteen of us making the car groan.

My water glass was purple. Not a tornado color at all.

Worst day of my career, Dave, the COO had said. He must have left too by now, though he probably got a payout, and I understood I could be happy for him. I could be happy for anyone, even Jimmy, even myself, given the right circumstances.

The ice water was condensing against the warmth of my hand, and Jimmy's note fluttered against the refrigerator door.

Maybe the final wisps of the air from the balloon were trapped between a fold of latex, air that had become even smaller as it froze.

Maybe with the right application of pressure or temperature, we could puff it up once more, and do it without having to go on tornado watch. Maybe if we were smart and careful, it could expand again.

THE EMPATHY CHART

You and I were at a party somewhere when we first met, and first we had to talk about the weather, as people do. We were living in Denver, Colorado, where the mountains let out their breath and bleed into the plains, and we'd long since come to accept, if not fully gotten used to, the ways the days could turn from blazing sunshine to hail as thick and big and hard as a nickel in a matter of hours. *It will get up to 81 on Sunday and Monday it's meant to snow!* we'd say, repeating the forecast with a false incredulity. (It seemed impossible with the blue Sabbath skies, but we dug out our boots and puffy ski coats anyway, and by the evening the wind had picked up and the cloudline was advancing from the northwest.)

You, like everyone I know who has lived or currently does live here, are an armchair meteorologist. I am too. When I am at home alone and hear the wind picking up, I think of your gentle *don't worry* look.

"Stormy from the east," my husband, Matt, says, coming in from the balcony where he was taking a phone call. I don't know why he needed privacy for it, but I don't ask.

Since we met at friend of a friend's springtime party, I am almost always thinking of you. You are not my husband. Matt is my husband. When I am at work, when I am walking to work, when I am walking home from work, when I am watering my plants on my balcony, when I am talking to Matt, I am thinking of you. When I am at work looking at numbers and partitioning them into their individual spreadsheet cells— in the cells the numbers are boxed but the box makes them more pliable; they can be tabulated and sorted and formulas can be applied—I am also thinking of you. The numbers react differently than humans who are boxed. I am in my box, you are in yours, and Matt is in his, but we keep spilling over. It's not clear if you and I think we are two halves meant to be joined or some other decimal. I can't be a true half, because I'm already joined to someone else, Matt. Maybe there's some theory of halves that would allow both, but I don't know it. I'm an analyst so I don't really speculate. I'm more about firm results.

It's a clear day in Denver when I am walking home from my office in downtown to the townhouse I share with Matt in a nearby neighborhood. It's one of those pretty, yellow-gray June afternoons lit hot gold where the sun shines uninterrupted by trees or buildings, and warmly pewter in the shade.

Light, also, is not good at being boxed, always shifting and licking at the edges.

At work, my boss, Kate, is a wreck. We've just been through layoffs, and we lost so many (Michael, Sabine, Christian, others), and Kate either doesn't know or doesn't seem to care that she is bound to be next. She hired me, and we're not friends exactly, but we have that particular kind of familiarity that comes with seeing one another five days a week for a number of years.

I walk and I wonder how I can see you again. So far, we've only met in public. The first time was at that party, and we both drank too much and you kept asking me about my work, about what I do with numbers and data, and I kept asking you what you wanted to know. If you had asked me the same question, at the party, or at the coffee shop dates that came after, I would have said, *Courage. I need to know how to find courage.* Remember, at that party, all those market people. Oil and gas. Financial services.

Remember how you were trying to relate but they didn't care about your stories.

Remember how you didn't notice their indifference towards you, even though when you spoke there was a sheen. You drew me in, if no one else. I pushed for your number and then I called, which you didn't expect. I would never ask for numbers if I didn't intend to use them.

You know now that in the work I am paid for, I put points on graphs, and draw correlations. This is also the work that calls me. I am lucky in this way, though I don't like particularly to discuss luck. Generally, I am very careful and my numbers are better than a crystal ball.

Walking, I'm almost home, and I'm distracted by Kate, by you. I take a wrong step.

My ankle rolls on the concrete.

I don't fall, at least not completely. Half in and half out of the light. *Okay, okay,* I think. *It hurts, but it's okay.* I limp the rest of the way home. I pretend it's a sprain. I don't have a bad ankle necessarily, but there is an old injury on the right side, the hurt side, and I pretend it is this, at first. A once-torn ligament could be quick to unravel, I think.

The walking does not go well, and I stop every other step to balance on the opposite foot and take a rest. The other alternative is to fold onto the sidewalk and cry. I'm maybe forty steps from home. I think about calling Matt to bring the car, but getting to a place where he could safely park the car is almost as many steps.

I take a step, breathe, take a step, rest.

After I get to the door, swearing at my key, which has never fit without some jiggling, I collapse. I'm still trying to pretend it's okay because I am not ready for the alternative.

Matt half carries and half drags me up the stairs to our bedroom. Our townhouse is a very vertical space.

"Water the plants?" I ask him, and nod my head towards the balcony.

"Of course," he says. He props a pillow under my foot to elevate it. It throbs, feels heavy and light at the same time, which I identify as the feeling of uselessness. If it is broken, for one, it will be harder to see you, even though I am not actually seeing you all that often.

Matt returns with ice and aspirin. He props me up on pillows. He buys into the idea of a sprain and he does his best to reassure me.

"Elevate," he says.

"I am elevating," I say.

He waters the outdoor plants like I have asked, and makes some phone calls while I read a magazine. He brings me dinner in bed. I read some more, and he makes more phone calls. We watch a movie together, and I fall asleep.

*

By the next day, when my foot has not bruised but is incredibly sensitive to touch, we visit the clinic. I am x-rayed and the x-ray reveals the fissure in the bone on the pinky-toe side of my foot, though it doesn't look like much—a streak of watery gray where there should be solid white.

Still, I am given a hard cast from toe to knee. The fiberglass wrapper is powder pink. I pick the color from a limited palette. Matt is angry, now, disbelieving. He is angry because he thinks I should have been paying more attention. He is disbelieving that I could be so careless to destroy—this is the word he uses, *destroy*—a part of my body. I think he is also angry that I've put this burden of care on him. He doesn't say this, but we both know it is going to be more than watering the plants.

For perhaps the first time in my life, I'm a statistical outlier. Annually, only 1.8 percent of Americans will break a bone. In comparison, an annual 5 percent will visit Disneyland. I have never been to Disneyland. When I tell Matt these statistics, he says "What?" and I know he is thinking this comparison doesn't track, but I think it does.

In her office, my doctor says I have a 45 percent chance of not having to have surgery, and I ask her if she is being specific, or just putting it at some point under fifty that seems acceptable to patients.

"I'm not quite sure what you mean," she says.

She sounds just like Matt, and for a moment, I lose all hope.

*

It was a Friday when I was wrapped in the pink fiberglass, so I have the weekend to think about it. Matt is catching up on the work he missed shuttling me between x-ray and ortho (my new language, medical shorthand), and he is quietly tapping on his laptop.

On Sunday, I say to him as gently as I can, *It's laundry day* and he looks at me in a way I can't parse.

It's not that Matt is cruel or lazy or incapable. He lived for a long time without me and presumably ate from clean dishes and wore clean underwear. I think there is a certain kind of man who is easy to forget his life before being coupled, but that's not what bothers me. What bothers me is how indignant he is. It feels like he wants an apology, and I have already decided I will not give one.

With the laundry, I knock the hamper over with a crutch and I sit on the floor and sort the colors. I wrap each pile up in a sweatshirt or stuff it into a pillowcase to make it easier for him. He's downstairs so I text him instead of hollering down the stairwell, *If you can just run these all in cold, and then dry on low.* I have separated out the delicates, thinking I'll find a way to do these on my own because it feels inexplicably hard to explain how to wash my bras over text, and I don't want to ask him to come up to me and I don't want to go down to him. It's only laundry, but suddenly the balance of our marriage seems to be dangling with the hang dries.

*

Monday comes, and I decide to take the days off of work that my doctor had said I should. I am good at following directions. The ortho's assistant has written me a note, and I feel ashamed at first, like a teenager looking for an excuse, but then I scan it and send it to HR anyway so they can document my request.

I am thinking of you, but I don't contact you because I don't want your pity. I have enough of my own.

In an email, Kate makes it very, very clear that she is annoyed. I email back. *I promise I am more annoyed than you are. I'm working remote, so call if you need anything. Frustrating all around.* I make an entry in one of my sheets. I'm starting to conceive of a different way to map personality—instead of a Myers-Briggs or a Herrmann Brain Dominance Instrument, I think of graphing empathy for self and for others. Then I close this file and start working on something for work, for Kate.

*

As I am at home, I elevate my leg, I think of my empathy chart, and on the second day, I call you on your mobile.

"Hey, so kind of out of the blue, but want to come over to my house?" I say. "I have a surprise."

You say your morning is clear, and you'll be at my place in twenty.

When you ring my bell, I realize I'll have to get all the way down the stairs, and while I grab my crutches, it's mostly painful sliding. I realize I haven't had a shower. I realize I've invited you into my home— of course I realized this when I called, but it still jolts me: this is the home I share with my husband. Matt is at work. I realize I have done this because I know you will say *yes*, and I am using my broken bone as a way to see you.

This is not like me, and on the last bumps of steps towards the front door, I am unmoored. I remind myself I have weighed the risks. I remind myself that I am unhappy with an unhappiness much bigger and much harder to deal with than a broken ankle. The ankle will heal, eventually. Even if it does require surgery after the twenty-nine more days until the cast comes off, there is a plan in place.

The door to the townhouse I share with Matt opens onto a foyer that leads to the living room.

Matt and I do not have a plan, other than the usual of going forward, of trying to stay married.

You are in my home in your only slightly crumpled suit.

We've never been alone like this. Mostly we've flirted on the margins, or gripped hands as we look away from the public. Seeing you in my doorway makes my stomach flip, but I try my best to hide it.

You, like me, might be a little queasy with nervousness, but you are not letting it show either. Your face, like my face, is a zero. And what is a zero. A hen's egg before its shape is made un-uniformly oval by a chicken's cloaca. Or, an invention of the Babylonians. The **O** of your slightly open mouth. The halo made as rocket fuel burns.

I say *Hello, come in come in* and turn and start crutching away from you. I'm trying to look expert on the crutches, though I have been mostly reclining or crawling because the crutches make my hands and armpits hurt. With my back to you, the rubber tip at the bottom of the left crutch catches a throw rug, and I topple, near my coffee table.

For a moment, it is very quiet.

A zero is a hurricane's eye.

And then you are on the floor with me, and then you are kissing me and then you are taking off my clothes and then you are angling, and then you are pushing the coffee table to make more room and to be careful of the cast and then you are inside of me.

It seems like it lasts for a very, very long time.

Afterwards I don't fall all the way asleep, because I have better control than that. I do almost doze for a few minutes and then I'm alert again.

You are the one who is snoring, whose snores have snapped me into full consciousness.

On my empathy chart, I am not sure where you would fall.

I wake you and you help me up from the floor. You help me into the shower, after you have helped me into the latex bag that is supposed to keep my cast dry. So far, it is working. You come into the stall with me and wash my hair. You hold my arm so I can balance, you soap me and rinse me. Then you towel me off, you change the bed sheets even though you and I were not in them together, it's just you seem to know how good the fresh cotton will feel against my scrubbed skin.

"Water the plants?" I ask. It's summer. It's hot.

"Of course," you say.

*

By the next week, I'm back at work, but only every other day. I could do every day, from an energy perspective, but the shower is an obstacle, especially without you. The shower feels dangerous, both hard and slippery. Matt is not indifferent, but he doesn't do what you did and come inside. He has his own work, his own stress. He's not an unkind person as a rule, but he is rigid. He likes routines as much as I like my formulas. Sometimes when I make a graph, I'll choose the setting in Excel for a smooth trendline. I would never choose that for Matt. He's all edge. That's not a criticism. I have loved that about him.

When my mother was still alive, the shower was one of the first things Matt and I insisted on when she moved into her new apartment— we replaced the old tub and overhead nozzle with a setup that could be accessed with a wheelchair, though she was not in a wheelchair then and never would be. But I wanted her to be able to glide right in, and I deeply feared her falling.

"People over sixty-five are the most likely to have an accident in the home," I had reminded my mom.

"And why do you think that is?" she had asked.

"That's why we are replacing the tub," I had said. "It's dangerous."

"It's not the damn tub," my mother had said. "It's because we are always here. If seniors were at the bar all the time, it would be the same rate. Probably more."

"She has a point," Matt had said, but my mother sent him a look that said *shut up*.

Defiance was something I loved about my mother. She always took my side if someone else intervened in our arguments, even when I didn't need her to, and even when I was wrong. My dad had left when I was very small and I had no memory of him. I wasn't sure if he was alive, but it felt like he was not. It felt like it didn't matter one way or the other.

One thing I notice, when I'm on crutches and navigating the office, is how many automatic doors are broken. Press the button, and nothing. Another thing I notice, when I'm on crutches, is how invisible I am, how people pass right by because I am slow-moving, because I have a foot wrapped in pink fiberglass. And I also notice how I am a target for the other invisibles—the men who would catcall me on my walks to and from work now see an obvious weakness. I wonder if they remember how I've told them that no, I don't have change, no, I don't want to talk for a while, and no, I won't smile—*don't tell people what to do with their own fucking face*, I said to one once—and now they are persistent in a new way.

In the short space crutching between an Uber and my building elevator, I honor every request for change that is asked, I grant every smile. I move like a slow, sloping graph. I'm the exploded piece of the pie chart that gets dismissed as anomaly. I've never felt so vulnerable in my life.

Maybe the thing my mother was saying was that older folks are not just home all the time, but they are home alone. An injury is hopefully temporary, but in a way, I wish I had understood when she was alive, I start to get why my mother was so angry at our offers of help. It wastes so much time, waiting for someone. Of course she pulled out the stepladder to reach her gravy tureen when we were there for the last Thanksgiving, when she insisted on cooking. Of course she insisted on cooking. Sometimes you want something done, and want it done your way, even if that means taking twenty minutes to hobblingly hang up your bras in the laundry room.

That last Thanksgiving, after she had drug out the ladder while I was in the bathroom, I gasped when I saw her on it. "Just let me help you," I had said, and she gave me that same defiant look she usually reserved for Matt.

I should have spent less time chastising her and taking things over and more time spotting her as she made her slow climbs. I am so, so sorry that I was short with her about the gravy tureen. A few months later she was dead, water pooled in her lungs. Would more steps on the ladder have saved her from that?

*

In the office, our COO, Dave, and also my boss, Kate, remain irritated with me and my every other day schedule, which they perceive as me not sucking it up hard enough. I'm not surprised about this from Dave, and he's also never liked it when people work from home, but I am surprised about Kate. Kate is scattered with pain—we all know that Jimmy, her soon-to-be ex-husband, served her with papers but we all pretend like we don't—and I start to wonder what was really going on in their house. I start to wonder why she is being cruel. She was never like that.

Every other day when I am working from home, you are meeting me at the door. You are peeling off my clothes. You are holding my tongue in your mouth. You are washing my hair and drying my body.

I have a new data project. My new project is calculating how many times I can sleep with you before Matt finds out. The algorithm I have begun to chart out is lovely but inconclusive.

After we have sex, you water my balcony plants. The dahlias are exploding, orange and yellow. I'm not sure if Matt doesn't notice or doesn't care. I could put our sex on a chart, desire of you against indifference toward my husband, but I don't.

*

In the office, on a day I am there, Kate is let go. There is a feeling like the one when tabulated data shows an unwanted but unavoidable result. There is nothing that can change it, besides to start over.

Kate does not want to start over; Kate is already starting over in the wake of her divorce. Kate goes to the supply closet to find a box to pack her stuff, and Dave follows her. I want to follow her, too, but I am so slow and so conspicuous on the crutches.

I'm not sure what Dave says to her, but Kate reappears without a box, grabs her purse and heads for the elevator.

*

I have another new project. My new project is calculating how many times I can sleep with you before I fall in love with you.

*

It's not that I dislike Matt, but when I think of you, it seems impossible that I would have chosen Matt. Of course, I didn't know you existed, and Matt was so predictable. Matt felt so safe. Now that I know you better, it's the messy, unchartable, ungraphable, unmatrixable-ness that draws me to you. The way you work the shampoo in, even though my hands work just fine. The way you bring me lunches made with broccoli and kale and figs, high calcium, bone-building foods, you say. The way you clean the toes on my broken foot with a washcloth, and then you pinch each toe as you are drying with another washcloth.

"My toenails haven't grown on that side," I say, "But I've clipped the other side twice."

"It's okay," you say.

My newest projects.

How many times.

*

It's you who takes me to get the cast removed, not Matt. I tell him Kate is picking me up, and then Matt is slow getting out of the house in the morning and my heart is thundering that you'll pull up and our little boxes will break, but this doesn't happen.

After the technician cuts through the layers of wrapping and my skin is in the air for the first time, I expect to be elated but I am not. My foot is lumpy, swollen. I go back to the exam room, fiberglass gone, but still on crutches. I am fitted for a walking boot, but I can't walk in it. The pressure is excruciating.

You take me home, and you stay the day with me. We practice walking, while I lean against your shoulder. By the time you leave, a full hour before the earliest that Matt would ever be home, I am hobbling on my own. I am faster than I have been in over a month. On the empathy chart, you've scored so high I wonder if I need to reevaluate the input methodology.

When you leave, I decide to take a trip to the mailbox to post my growing stack of outbound mail. It's slow going and I am leaning on a cane, but I make it there and back. My whole leg tingles with the waking up of muscles and nerves and gentle pressure on the knitting of the bone, and it is a true feeling of freedom.

When Matt comes to the townhouse, while I am slow, I am watering the plants on my own, but he snatches the watering can out of my hands, saying that I don't need to push too hard on my first day.

I think of my mother and how at her funeral I checked my work email and answered a text from Kate.

"Give it back," I say to Matt, even though I am leaning on the cane. "Give it back to me."

He hands the can over, goes downstairs, and I tip it until it is empty, and then I keep up the motion of watering the plants, long after the watering can is dry. I think of my charts, my flowers, my foot, and I think of you. I think of how it's maybe not about halves or zeros at all, and it looks suddenly like the sky will crack with hail, the wind picking up and I'm outside, exposed, with my cane and my can.

Let it come, I think, *just let it come.*

WISH IN THE OTHER

In my life then, working at my office, I'd say there was this element of always being on edge about what would happen next like in a video I'd seen of teenage boys throwing smoke bombs down a canyon in Oregon. The shaky recording cuts out just after the spot where the wispy smoke begins to rise, but while the potassium nitrate has burst from its container, it's still encased between the rock walls of the canyon, and this is the most dangerous part, lit sparks loose in the dry valley. It was like how I figured my face must have looked when my boss, Kate, fired me: a slow smolder.

In the online video I could sort of see how everything would play out and also kind of not see anything, and while the boys must have eventually walked away from the ridge and gone back to their campsite or their car, when I first watched it, I already knew that it was not many frames away from the emergence of disaster. The boys are reckless and wide-eyed, like if they just had thrown a little harder, they would have hit their real target, like they would have known what they were throwing toward.

I was in my apartment when I saw the news report of the unintentional blaze—hot, dry conditions, a lighter passed back and forth, the fire igniting the forest floor then burning through the understory of the forest and up the canyon walls. I'd grown up in and still lived in Denver, and I'd never been to Oregon before, but it looked like a beautiful place, even with the hillsides glowing wrong and the river water so hot, it must have been bubbling through the bowl of the Columbia Gorge.

*

It was hard to know what to do with Cale when he called. We'd both been out of college for a few years, and when he contacted me, it was in the first week of losing my job. I'd been finished with school for much longer than Cale because he had gone on to do a PhD. I had some money saved, but I was considering moving back in with my mom—she'd offered, and honestly, besides me keeping up some kind of appearance of being an adult, there was no reason for us to live apart. It had been just us two since my dad left. My dad wasn't supposed to leave her, but that's what he wanted. I didn't want to leave her, but that's what I was supposed to do.

"I'm sure you'll find another job soon," my mom said over the phone, and I hoped she was right, but I learned a long time ago not to pin too much hope on anything. My mom, when she was in a mood, used to say, *Well, you can shit in one hand and wish in another and see which one fills up first.*

I think it had been close to a year since I had really talked with Cale. He was a math guy, and he'd ridden that through multiple scholarships. Even before I lost my job, I had mentioned wanting to go back to my mom's house to him.

"Yeah, man, it's not a problem *per se*, it's just optics. Like with girls, it doesn't look good," he said.

I was pretty sure I had never given a fuck about optics, whatever that even was.

"I don't date girls," I said.

"Oh shit," he had said. "This might be too heavy for right now."

I heard party sounds in the background. What I didn't get to say in that last conversation before Cale hung up was that I meant *women*. That a girl is a child. That the females in my life were only girls in the past tense unless they were, in fact, children. Probably he would have said something about me being hung up on the semantics of it, but I'd been raised by a single mom, and I saw how men treated her, and somewhere along the line I had taken a vow to be better. And I didn't get to tell him that I didn't appreciate his homophobia.

When Cale called this time, he did not sound sober at all. "Like if I could just crash with you for a few days? You still have your place? You didn't move back in with your mom? Right?"

Yes, I still had my place, I told him. *No*, I didn't move back in with my mother, at least not yet. *Sure*, he could stay with me for a few days.

"Where are you?" I asked. He'd done his BS in Chicago, his master's in Massachusetts, and had finally landed in California for his doctorate and had stayed on, working in a lab. Last I had heard from him, he loved the lab and the undergraduates.

"I'm like a little over halfway home," Cale said. "Staying at a friend's in Salt Lake. Well, friend of a friend."

Salt Lake City was still eight hours away from Denver by car. I wondered if he had talked to his dad but I figured not.

"I'm going to text you the address of where I am," he said, slurring at the end, *eye ammm*. "And then I am going to go to bed. And then when I wake up, I hope you will be here. I really really really really really need you to be here. Please, Laird." He coughed.

"Okay," I said. "Don't forget the text or I won't be able to find you."

"The text?" he said.

"Text the address," I said. "Maybe see if there's mail or something you can get the address off of. Or drop a pin. But I need the address."

"I got you," he said. "I'll go get the mail."

"Charge your phone," I said, but he had already hung up.

I put down my cell, and I rummaged in my apartment—change of clothes, toothbrush, stuffed into a bag. I filled all of my water bottles. It was almost nine in the evening, and I'd meant to read for a while and then go to sleep, but instead I brewed a pot of coffee, dumped it into a thermos, and brewed another cup for my to-go mug. Into the bag went a banana, a couple of string cheeses, granola bars, and an apple. I took my morning vitamins. I took a piss. I waited to leave until my phone finally dinged with Cale's text, and then I put the address into my GPS. I figured even if a number was transposed, I'd get close enough. I figured that by the time I got to him, he'd be sobering up.

I didn't know if Cale was reaching for me or if he was just reaching. I double-checked that I had my wallet and my phone charger, and I took the coffee and the water and the food to my car. On the way out of town, I topped off the tank and, on a whim, ran my old Honda through the automatic car wash. Inside, while I waited for the machine to soap and rinse and soap and rinse again, I called my mom and left a message and told her I was taking a road trip to see Cale, and that everything was fine. I called Kevin, Cale's dad, and thanked him for the birthday card he had sent months ago and asked if he had talked to Cale recently. *Anyway, call me back*, I said.

My car was cool and glistening after the wash, or at least it would be until the water dried. After that it would be a matte burgundy color with a scratch down the side and a pitted windshield, but for now my coffee was hot, my water cold, my ride shiny, and my gas tank full. I turned to head west on I-70, and wondered if this was something Cale would do for me.

*

I wanted to have some great experience of the open road—a young man who has lost his job and is setting out to claim his oldest friend, his friend who was everything to him not even a decade ago, his friend whom he would once do anything for, a friend who had never needed much from him, but now the friend does need, so the young man is barreling down the interstate, alternating between coffee and water, eating a banana to stay awake, slapping himself to stay awake, eating a granola bar to stay awake, doing jumping jacks at a rest station to stay awake, eating a string cheese to stay awake, getting gas to stay awake, thinking of every painful moment he can conjure from his life to stay awake while he drives because though his friend has not said so, he would not have called if he was not in over his head. The young man does not know if it's smoke or water or something else covering his friend, but he felt the muffling of his voice, heard the *please*, heard the *really really really need you*, and so now he is punching the accelerator and chugging the coffee and what's left of the water and watching the odometer tick through the miles, and he is balancing being safe against going faster while he tries to bounce a message off the sky *I'm coming, I'm coming*. But mostly, it was just dark highway.

*

Silent for hours, my GPS spoke again as I reached the outskirts of Salt Lake. I turned her voice off. It was almost six in the morning, the edge of daybreak. I was very, very tired, so I pulled over at a truck stop, set the alarm on my phone, and slept for just over an hour in the back seat, until Cale's message dinged.

Just woke up, where are you?

20 minutes, I tapped back.

In the truck stop I gassed up, pissed, and got a refill of coffee. Splashed water on my face. There was a voicemail from my mom, sounding chipper, but nothing from Kevin, Cale's dad. On my way back to my car, a trucker offered me something to keep me awake, a translucent red lozenge in his outstretched hand, but I turned it down. He said to me that I looked like I needed it. I said I didn't think he was wrong.

Back on the highway, I listened to the radio as the GPS voice guided me to a tumbledown house in a generally nice neighborhood. On the radio the community in Oregon wanted consequences for the boys. There was still a wreath of smoke through the valley, and the fire was not contained. "I don't care if they are just kids," one interviewee said. "They should go to jail and they should pay."

I parked and clicked off the ignition and the story stopped. Before I could knock on the door, it opened, and there was Cale. I hadn't seen him in three years. He had always been thin, but now he was a scraggled kind of skinny, and he smelled worse than I did.

Beyond him, through the doorway, I could see a mess of bodies passed out on couches, on the floor, and maybe someone upright in the kitchen, or maybe a dog licking the countertops.

And his arms around me. "I didn't think you'd come!" he said. He was crying and his snot was on my shirt.

I pulled him to me. "Hey, you'd come for me."

"I'd try," he said, gulping air. "I promise I would try."

"You would," I said, turning my face away.

*

He only had a daypack, so in a minute it was back to the car. We stopped at McDonald's on the way out of town, and I talked the cashier into refilling my water bottles and my coffee thermoses. Cale had three sausage McMuffins with cheese, and I thought that was a good sign, that he was hungry. I had a biscuit and a hash brown, and I thought of the trucker's red lozenge and that maybe I should have accepted it. I was the dazed kind of tired, but Cale seemed worse than me. He leaned heavily on the sticky tabletop.

"Are you coming down?" I asked him as he finished his last sandwich.

"I'm not sure," he said. "It's like California is just some kind of memory. Kind of remember being in a van, kind of remember talking to you, but I woke up about 2 a.m. and thought it was a dream, but I saw my text to you and went to wait at the window, and when you were actually there, it was *wow*. Laird, like really, *wow*."

"*Wow!*" I played along.

Cale spilled ketchup down the front of his shirt, and I took a deep breath. Eight more hours back to Colorado. He definitely could not drive, and I wasn't sure if I could.

At the counter I ordered more breakfast sandwiches, two Big Macs, and some fries, and asked the cashier again to top off my coffee. The food would be cold before we wanted or needed it, but we had to stay awake, and I did not want to stop more than necessary.

*

By the time we got to Grand Junction, Colorado—about thirty miles past the Utah state line—I was really dragging. I pulled over for gas and breathed in the fumes, hoping for a jolt, but there was nothing but stink. Cale was passed out in the back seat. He had eaten both of the cold hamburgers and then crashed. Outside of my quick nap at the truck stop, I had been awake for close to forty hours.

It was late morning and while I waited for the tank to fill, Cale's dad called.

I meant to be cool, but I was exhausted and hungry from not having eaten real food and worried about my friend, and I told him everything. Cale was strung out, passed out. I was running on barely any rest. I had lost my job and wasn't totally broke yet but definitely on my way. I was going to move back in with my mom to save money, but also I wanted to move back in with my mom because I missed her. Cale didn't look good—it had been hours, and even if he was sleeping, he was still wasted.

I heard Kevin typing. He told me to rest, that he had made an arrangement at a hotel, and he read me the address.

"I think I can make it the rest of the way to Denver," I said.

"Sleep a bit," he said. He was insisting. "Even if it is only a few hours. Get home safe. Can you come here first? Drop him off?"

It was like we were in high school again. I listened to Kevin, always had. I wished Kevin was my dad too.

"Can you call my mom?" I said, surprised at how my voice broke, and then not surprised.

"Sure, Buddy," Kevin said. "I'll call her right when we hang up."

*

The hotel was not some roachy thing that I would have done on my own dime but a nice place. I had to almost drag Cale through the lobby, but because he was my oldest friend, I refused to be embarrassed, even though people were staring at us. When I got him to the room, he was babbling and feverish, and I was glad we were not in the car.

In the video of the boys throwing smoke bombs, they are egging one another on. By the ninth or tenth time I'd watched it, I was almost sure they both knew what a bad idea it was but they did it anyway. In the news updates since the morning, the state of Oregon had announced they would attempt to try the boys as adults and seek a prosecution for destruction of public property.

In the hotel room Cale snored in his bed. I took a shower and I tried to relax. I ate the last breakfast sandwich. It was cold and the cheese was congealed and the bread soggy. I drained one of my water bottles. I pissed.

I crawled into the clean hotel sheets, and the horizontal feeling was welcome, but I couldn't sleep with Cale in the room with me. I wondered if he would be hungry when he woke up. I wondered if he drank coffee. I wondered if I was the first person he called or the last. I wondered if he would be angry when I took him to his dad's. I wondered if I would take him to his dad's—maybe my place for a day or two would be better.

I wondered what he was coming off of, and I wondered if there was something I should be looking for, like tremors or delirium or something else. He kept snoring, and I was glad because I could hear him breathe.

*

It was 4 p.m. when I jolted awake. Cale was still in the other bed, tangled in the sheets. I had texts from my mother and three missed calls from Kevin. I had that urgent feeling of being late for work. I remembered that I had been fired. I showered quickly, put on my one change of fresh clothes, and made hotel-room coffee.

It took me another forty minutes to get Cale awake. He reeked. When I pulled back the bedsheets, there was a ring of yellow, so I hauled him into the bathroom. He was barely responsive but once he was stripped, I folded him into the tub and turned on the shower, running it hot, running it cold. Either temperature, he sat and turned his face to the stream of water.

"Are you okay?" I asked.

"No," he said.

I put Cale in the hotel robe and tucked him in the dry bed. I made him drink some water. I was worried about leaving him, but my phone GPS indicated a Target only three miles away, so I raced there to get clean clothes and snacks. Underwear, sweatpants, socks, and a shirt. Three protein shakes. More bananas. Bottled water. Three packaged sandwiches and a large bag of almonds. I ate the almonds by the handful on the way back to the hotel, chasing the nuts with one of the protein shakes. I felt a little bit better.

We checked out of the hotel, Cale clean and wearing the sweats and underpants and socks. The clothes he was wearing stank so bad I left them in the room, and I put twenty bucks on his bed for housekeeping. I figured they'd seen worse than rotten jeans and pee, and it was the last of the cash that I had budgeted for the trip, but still.

It was close to 6 p.m. by now, with four more hours to Denver. I texted my mom and Kevin:

Leaving Grand Junction see you soon I love you both.

*

When Cale and I were about the same age as the boys in the smoke bomb video, we'd go down to Kevin's basement and smoke pot, and we tried whatever else we could get our hands on, which truthfully wasn't as much as we pretended it to be. Two misfit kids trying on a bad-boy identity, falling asleep to *Lethal Weapon 3* for the hundredth time.

Maybe he was more into our limited drug scores than I was—it's just as hard to trust any memory as to pull one up. I know we weren't the kind of kids who set off alarm bells, who set things on fire, ourselves or a forest, even by accident.

My mom, his dad, us two, we made a kind of family, and Cale and I did the kinds of things kids who haven't had it too hard do. Kept our grades up. Didn't mouth off too much. Didn't get caught. It had been hard when my dad left, but that was so long ago, I had stopped, or at least tried to stop, caring. Everything seemed fine but maybe Cale was more like those smoke bomb boys than I knew. Maybe he was tinder ready to be lit, maybe he was burning and I didn't know how to see it, maybe he was already ash.

*

"I can't sleep," Cale said from the back seat when we had about another hour to go.

I was trying to decide if I was going to take him to my place for a little bit to chill or if I should drop him at Kevin's.

"You've been sleeping since last night," I said. The cruise control, one of the few things that worked correctly in my aging car, was set to seventy-five, but it felt like we were going very, very slowly.

"Do you have a joint?" Cale asked.

"No, man," I said. "There's water back there, though. And bananas and a sandwich and a protein shake."

"Fuck you, Laird, and fuck you and your fucking ba-*na*-nas."

I decided I would take him to Kevin's.

"Sorry," he said. "I'm fried."

"Drink some water," I said.

"Laird, bro, I love you, but also fuck off with the water already."

Yes, definitely taking him to Kevin's.

We were close now, coming in through the suburbs. Cale had crashed out again, only to wake just as Denver started to peek through the plains. He told me he was hungry and that he had to shit. I took this as a good sign, the body waking up. Unless he had a stash with him, he had been off whatever he was on for almost twenty-four hours. It was a start.

We pulled over at a rest stop, and I followed him into the stall, because I was not going to let him run. I was also not going to let him buy a red lozenge off of a trucker. I texted my mom as I waited.

"I can't go with you loitering out there," he said.

"Yes, you can," I said.

Almost home. Let's talk about me coming back to your place, or we get a new place. I don't care about the optics.

Optics? she responded immediately.

I heard Cale's bowels loosen in a sudden way. He groaned. The stench was immediate and terrifying, even for a rest stop.

The way it looks. I don't care how it looks.

There were more sounds from the stall, Cale's voice, and Cale's body. When he finally emerged, he looked deflated.

"Are you sure you don't have a joint?" he said.

"Positive," I said. I washed my hands in the cold rest stop water for the third time. I'm not a germophobe but the space felt dirty. "I'm not sure a joint would help you, really."

"God. I fucking hate you right now, Laird."

"I know," I said. "Wash your hands."

"You are the worst. You are the worst person I have ever met in my life," he said. He smashed the tap and the water ran. He soaped up with the grainy powder soap from the dispenser. He lathered in a dramatic way to ensure that I saw.

He was misunderstanding me. I didn't want to police him, only get him home.

Okay!! My phone dinged with my mom's text.

After he rinsed, he raised his leg and kicked the air dryer, but by the time it started up in a whir, he was already headed for the car, fingers dripping.

I turned over the ignition in the Honda for what I hoped would be the last time in a long time. On the radio a journalist was discussing how the boys in Oregon thought they were getting away with something but they were wrong. They were getting away with nothing after creating their own documentation. No one could say how long the forest would keep burning, how long the river would bubble.

Cale was asleep again. A light snow began to fall, and I cursed it because I did not have good tires. By the time we were in Denver proper, it was all floppy, wet flakes, and I wanted to be off the roads. I lurched into my apartment building's garage because it was the closest—I knew Kevin was waiting, but I couldn't do another twenty minutes to his house and then come back to mine.

It took some effort to get Cale out of the back seat. I listened to my car's cooling engine tick. For the second time today, I half-dragged him to bed. I wondered if he would piss in his sleep again, and then I decided I didn't care. My mattress was old.

In my kitchen I cracked a beer and called my mom.

"I'm home," I told her, then drained the beer nearly empty. "I'm beat."

"Kevin's on the other line, hon, I'll conference you in."

The three-way conversation was short, and my mom and Cale's

dad decided they were coming over, even though I told them I had nowhere for all of us to sleep. Kevin said he'd bring an inflatable bed and my mom said, *Great.*

"I'll grab some extra sheets," she said.

When they arrived, with the air mattress, spare bedding, and a pizza, I wasn't sure who to fall into first. It was my mom who caught me, but Kevin's hand was there too.

Outside the snow was swirling harder, and when I blinked, it was like nothing changed at all since high school—it's me and Cale and my mom and Kevin and the smell of pepperoni.

When Kevin went to check on Cale, my mom went with him. Her hand laced in his.

"Does it smell like piss? He pissed the bed in the hotel," I'm trying to ask, but actually I'm just crying, I'm so tired.

"Nope," Kevin said. "I think he's good. You got him out of the woods. I've already researched inpatient treatment."

"Okay," I said. There was snot running down my face.

In another version the boys in Oregon would have just set off their smoke bombs in the backyard. That's probably what Cale and I would have done. We would have known we would get in trouble, but we'd also know there was no use trying to hide anything. Maybe by making the video they wanted to get found out. Maybe they didn't have the same kind of safety we had, to screw up in plain view of a parent. Maybe they thought they had to sneak around, and they never thought about the video being uploaded and used as evidence, and rather than YouTube hits, it was meant to be just for them.

I drank another beer, we ate some of the pizza. We bedded down, my mom and Kevin fully clothed on the squeaky air mattress, me in my jeans on the creaky couch. I was glad they were with me. I heard Cale snoring from my room.

I was too tired to wonder if them sleeping on the air mattress together was just a measure of practicality or if there was finally something happening between them. Now that I thought about it, I wasn't sure if I they were really holding hands earlier or not. I wondered if the boys in Oregon would actually end up in jail. It seemed unlikely. They were kids, and they weren't innocent, but children all the same. What if it would have been me and Cale in that canyon? Would we have used a cellphone to call 911 at the first rise of smoke instead of filming it? I could see how it had all gotten out of hand very quickly, and I could see that they should have sprinted for help, but it was hard for me to believe the boys actually wanted the forest to burn, if they had known what it meant.

PIVOT, FEATHER

In her apartment, Sabine sat on the sofa, between her current boyfriend and her former coworker. The boyfriend, whose real name was Ryan but went by Sebastian, lived in the apartment with her, and now every time she pronounced the first *S*, it felt like a hiss. The former coworker, Michael, had surprised her when he had called, and since they were both unemployed and being careful with money, she had invited him over instead of meeting him somewhere out.

She and Michael were talking about the office, and about how they should have known layoffs were coming. The management had waffled between supportive and distant. Sabine had lied to get the job, and Michael had a family connection, which now she thought didn't seem to matter either way.

Sebastian did not seem to be listening. He was wearing the new kind of earbuds, the ones without connective wires, and Sabine thought they looked stupid, hanging there, attached to nothing, but what really annoyed Sabine was that she knew Sebastian/Ryan could hear her through the earbuds, but he pretended that he could not. His leg was just barely touching hers. The sofa was the only place to sit in the apartment, and she didn't feel like she could move farther away, and Michael was already hugging the armrest. Every couple of minutes, Sebastian's pant leg would rustle up against hers, and it felt like a warning.

Before, Sabine had been working as a barista and making the collages she called bird-scapes—feather and glue and found bits—and she'd been helping Sebastian/Ryan with his own mixed-media work. From the beginning of the six months she'd had the cubicle job in an office, she'd barely had time to help her boyfriend, and she had also stopped caring. Not about art, she knew—even if she rose to VP at a corporation, she would always care about art—but she had stopped caring about *his* art, and in particular, she had stopped caring about being his helper.

His latest and, she thought, probably last installation piece was in the apartment's living room, hardly touched. It was panels of fabric, drizzled in candle wax, and then crumpled up while the wax was still hot so the wrinkles were bound together. Each was around a square yard, and there was a stack of close to forty. These were meant to be stitched together with thick, visible threads, heavy string, twine, or yarn, and the idea was to represent the unpredictable ways in which lives fold: *Even the same medium on the same material can produce very different results*, Sebastian's artist's statement read. All that was left was the actual stitching, which Sabine had once said she would do.

It had been difficult to describe to Sebastian how the office made her tired, even though the hours were not much longer and the work certainly less physical than being a barista. She would not say that either one was harder, but at her desk job, though she made a great deal more money, she also had far less autonomy, and that was a challenge.

"Actually, at work I spend a lot of time finishing up the last details of other people's projects," she had said, when she was again explaining why she was not going to stitch his panels. "It has shown me how important it is to me to work on my own things. I think that's what I liked about pulling coffee; each order was me, from start to finish."

"Not true," he had said. "You needed a customer there, to pay for it and to drink it. Otherwise, it would not have a reason to exist." He said this as a pronouncement.

Sebastian had some money from his parents, a large sum, but it continued to dwindle because he did not earn. He said he could always ask for more, if he needed to. There was a time when Sabine found this to be enviable. The night after she was let go from her office job, though, she had drunk too much wine and told Sebastian he should think about getting himself off of his parents' teat.

"What?" he had said.

"*Teat*," she had said. "Get off of it."

"I feel like I barely know you," he had said.

"It's mutual," she had said, angry that the first thing he'd done when she came through the door, her desk things in a cardboard box, was to get excited that now she would have time to finish the stitching. It was possible she had bared her teeth.

In the days that passed, she had offered to teach him to sew, and she had offered to borrow a machine from a friend or the makerspace at the library if he didn't want to do it by hand. She had told him that sewing was not actually all that hard, if you just wanted to join two items together. What was hard was making it look nice, and for his installation, looking nice was antithetical. Sebastian had said she was killing the collaborative nature of the project. She had said it wasn't a collaborative project; it had never been intended as a collaborative project. It was that he just didn't want to do the sewing.

Over several consecutive nights, they had fought.

"It won't take you that long," Sebastian had said. "And it will take your mind off being fired."

"It won't take you that long either," Sabine had said.

"But ten thousand hours of practice, that concept from that guy—I just think you could do it so much more quickly. It's a better use of time."

"Whose time," Sabine had asked. "And I don't have that much practice. My mom taught me the basics so I could fix my clothes when they ripped. I'm not a pro. I'm not so fast. I do not have ten thousand hours, and that's Malcolm Gladwell, and I need to look for a new job."

Now, from the sofa, sandwiched between him and Michael, Sabine eyed the stack of fabric squares. She knew Sebastian would never finish his project, and when she considered his catalog, meager as it was, she realized she'd always absorbed the domestic labor of it. He'd usually been game to scissor or cut or drizzle, but she'd been the one to heat the wax; she'd been the one to measure out the fabric panels in the first place; she'd been the one, in his prior project—dolls suspended from the ceiling, in different states of undress, some with missing limbs or heads, each with the strip of paper from a fortune cookie affixed to their delicate parts—who had gone at the torsos and in between their legs with a hot glue gun. She'd been the one who had visited the restaurant wholesaler and who had purchased the massive bag of cookies; she'd been the one to crack them open; she'd been the one who had sorted through the phrases and who had chosen the messages for the project.

The one who would be constant in happiness must frequently change.

You are known for being quick in action and decisions.

Be tactful: do not overlook your own opportunity.

She had also been the one who smoothed the papers, and had misted them with a spray of starch so the press would hold, ironing all the fortunes flat.

"Want to go to the coffee shop where I used to work?" Sabine asked Michael, from her middle place on the sofa. "I haven't been there in ages." She saw Sebastian frown, just slightly, but he kept swiping at whatever he had been swiping on his phone and listening through his earbuds, rustling his pant leg.

"Yes," Michael said, as he popped up from the sofa.

They walked out into the late autumn. The leaves had long since dried out and blown away, and the sidewalks felt matte, a simple palette of grays and browns, the red of Sabine's scarf a pretty accent.

When they opened the door to her old shop, none of her regulars were there, and the barista didn't know her.

"I honestly don't want any coffee," Michael said. "I only wanted to get out of your apartment. That guy is weird."

Sabine considered if she needed to defend her boyfriend about being called *that guy*, but she'd never defended Michael when Sebastian used it for him, *that guy you work with*, even though they both knew one another's names. She nodded and acknowledged. "It's awkward right now," she said.

They were both bored, without the office. For Michael, a college graduate who thought he was on his way to corporate greatness, it was a real crash of identity, but Sabine had wondered if the universe was sending her a message that it was time to return to her art.

For better or worse, do not misinterpret the intentions of a stranger.

Before they left the coffee shop, Sabine picked up an application. She folded the paper and stuffed it into her pocket as they walked toward a neighborhood park. The sun had come out, and though Sabine's shoes were not the greatest for the gravel trail, it was flat and so she didn't worry too much. They discussed their shared former boss Kate's erratic behavior, their peer Melissa's aloofness, and how it felt for Michael having to be fired by his own father, Dave, the COO. They decided there was some metaphor in there, only they didn't know what it was yet. Sabine said there was another metaphor with her between Michael and Sebastian on her sofa, but Michael didn't say anything. He kept his eyes on the gravel.

She and Michael had been flirting since they were both hired, right around the same time, in a period of rapid growth.

"Do you have a car, Michael?" she asked. "I'm sure you've told me before, but I can't remember."

"I have an old Camry," he said. "It runs okay. I was going to get a new one, but I'm holding off now."

"Do you want to help me look for feathers?" she asked, not sure how it sounded. "I used to make collages out of found feathers. Bird-scapes I called them. I sold one, once."

*

They drove toward the foothills of the Rockies, not far really, but Sabine again thought about her shoes. She wasn't dressed to be hiking the forests, but she hadn't wanted to go back to the apartment to change.

She started to tell Michael everything she could think to tell him about Sebastian, about how she thought his adopted name was ridiculous *His name is Ryan. Fuck, what the fuck,* she said, and the earbuds, and the way he tried to rope her into helping him with his installations, and she did not want to help with his installations.

"What fortune is that, starching and ironing the fortunes," she said. "When I get back, I am going to go into that apartment, and I am going to take my things, and I am going to call him *Ryan,* and I am going to tell Ryan that I am leaving," she said, and the force in her voice astonished her. The dark was starting to fall, but Michael just kept driving, and she wasn't sure if he was headed anywhere specific, but it didn't matter.

"I'll take you back whenever you want," he said. "You can stay at my house tonight, if you need to. My dad won't care; he knows you. The couch has a pullout bed on it."

It was such a simple offer, but it crushed Sabine, realizing how easy leaving Ryan would be, if she simply had a place to go. It had been her apartment initially, but she knew it would be hard to get him out, and she didn't think she could force him, at least not tonight.

"I could go to my mom's," she said, and she was not sure why she hadn't considered this before.

"I can take you," Michael said.

Sabine was crushed again. Her mother lived almost as far as they had driven, an hour's worth, in the opposite direction, but Michael didn't care, and he refused her offer of gas, saying he had gotten his unemployment check that morning.

"Yeah, so did I," Sabine said.

It was startling how much Michael's small kindnesses worked like grease on a stuck hinge, a slick of wax on a sticky window frame. Metal on metal, wood on wood—the grating feeling she had when she thought of how to handle her coupling with Sebastian, bone on bone, started to slip.

She and Michael decided to stop by the apartment, where she would pack her suitcase as fully and as quickly as she could, and then he'd drive her the rest of the way. She texted her mother, *Staying for a few days with you if that is cool.* Her mother texted back, *Sure, of course,* and said she could make dinner if Sabine could bring her a couple bottles of a nice white wine. Sabine thought that meant they'd probably drink the wine and then order pizza later, but that was okay with her.

It felt good to have an errand to do, something simple on top of the problem of leaving Ryan/Sebastian. It felt good to have the beginnings of a plan.

*

When Sabine first opened the door of the dark apartment, she thought he was gone, but then she saw him, sitting in almost the exact same place on the sofa. She was not sure if he was asleep or simply had his eyes closed. When he was very anxious, Sebastian could fall asleep on demand. The earbuds were still in place, and she thought she made out his phone loosely resting in one hand, but it was dark and she couldn't be sure. She stood very still in the entryway, waiting for the sound of a snore or any sign of movement, and then when there was nothing, she forced a cough. He did not stir, and she decided he was just ignoring her, since typically any small sound disturbed him.

Pulling her suitcase out of the closet, she packed quickly, some clothes, some things that were important to her, mementos and photos. Michael had asked if she was worried Ryan would trash her stuff, but she said she didn't think he was ambitious enough to make the effort, and even if he did, there was very little she had that was not replaceable. From her dresser, she took the photo of her and her mother when she was first born, a cheesy ceramic unicorn she'd had since she was a child, and a small clay sculpture that was meant to be an eagle but looked more like a penguin, given to her by a favorite uncle.

As she rolled her suitcase across the floor, the racket of the wobbly wheels on the worn-out hardwood would be enough to annoy the downstairs neighbors, but her almost ex-boyfriend did not budge. For a moment, Sabine wondered if he had had a heart attack or an aneurysm, but then she was sure she saw his eyelid flutter.

"Are you asleep," she asked, stopping just in front of the door to the apartment. When there was no answer, Sabine reached into her purse and dug for the small LED flashlight strung among her keys. She clicked it on and shone the light toward him.

"I said, 'Are you asleep,'" she repeated.

"Yes," he said.

She felt an anger rise that he would sit there, inert, while he had to have heard her packing, when there was no way he couldn't have heard the wheels of the suitcase. She wanted to leave—she was leaving—but it hurt her that he wouldn't at least fight a little to keep her.

"I'm not coming back, except to get the rest of my things," she said. "This is the end."

"I know," he said, and he kept his eyes closed to her flashlight.

For a moment, she had administrative concerns—the lease was in her name, the utilities—but she decided she could figure this out later.

Stacked near her feet were the fabric squares for the installation piece, and then the apartment and their entire relationship seemed terribly sad. How could she have loved someone who would just let her walk out, let her roll away with her suitcase with the lumpy wheels, let her go so easily, not even complaining that she'd left earlier with another man. How could she have loved someone who wouldn't try to sit her down and argue that they still had art to make together. Real art, not just picking up the administrative slack. Someone who could not offer her anything that showed whether she stayed or left was more telling than any of the fortunes. Someone who could not even open his eyes.

*

The drive to her mother's seemed very long. Sabine and Michael stopped at a liquor store to pick up the wine, and she puzzled for too long over what her mother might define as a "nice" white, at this point in her life, before settling on two mid-priced bottles of chardonnay, a pinot grigio outside of her current budget, and a box of sauv blanc.

She paid the total, and carried her purchase to Michael's car. The rest of the way to her mother's, they were silent, and she questioned if she should invite him in, if he would want to be invited in.

When they pulled up in front of the house, Michael didn't leave his intentions to question. He jumped out of the car, running around to the passenger side to open it for Sabine.

Who knocks at your threshold; do not ignore.

She had hot-glued this fortune to the crotch of one of the dolls, and she felt ashamed as it came back to her.

They approached her mother's steps, and the door was cracked open. Sabine called out, "Knock, knock," and her mother said, "Hey! Come in!"

The wine was put on ice, and Sabine immediately wished she'd thought to get flowers.

"This is Michael," she said. "We used to work together."

"Oh, honey," Sabine's mother said. "I'm so sorry. I'm Julie." She reached out her hand but then folded Michael into a hug. The kitchen smelled like oregano and garlic, and Sabine was relieved that there was actual cooking taking place. "Stay for dinner?" she asked Michael, and he caught Sabine's eye over Julie's head, asking permission.

"He'll stay," Sabine said. "Thanks, Mom. Smells great. You didn't have to do this."

"I know how a transition feels," she said. "Oh, Beenie, it's so good to see you."

Sabine winced at being called *Beenie* in front of Michael—it was the last two syllables of her name, and her mom over the years had called her first Bina and then Beenie—but she understood her mother was not trying to embarrass her. And she also realized, perhaps for the first time since she'd been on her own, that really, who cared. Her mother had an affectionate nickname for her. It meant she had a mother. It meant her mother had affection for her.

"Mike," Sabine's mother was saying, "listen, I'm not so traditional, but Beenie is here after just leaving SRyan—you know that's what I called him, SRyan—so no hanky-panky. You'll be in the living room, though you seem like a nice guy and no offense. Or you can go home. But I won't let you go home if you've been drinking. Not worth it, trust me. Wine? Yes? Great. Hand me your keys."

Michael reached into his pocket and dug out his keys, and Sabine's mother put them on the counter. Sabine let herself float into her mother's tendency to monologue, her mother's tendency to give advice. She had missed that about her mom, the way she was always so sure.

*

They did, eventually, finish dinner. A garlic-soaked chicken deglazed with the box wine—by the time it was ready, they'd worked their way through the bottles.

"No matter," Julie said, and laughed and laughed and laughed as the steam from the oven fogged her glasses.

Michael took over, inserting the meat thermometer and making a salad.

"Oh, you keep him," Julie said to Sabine. "A man who eats greens. Your father thought broccoli was a sign of the apocalypse."

Sabine didn't think of her father that often, and she certainly didn't think of him in terms of vegetables.

At some point, Julie dumped a heap of sheets and pillows in the living room and then hustled herself off to bed. Sabine helped Michael make up the couch before she turned to her childhood room. They'd never been intimate, but now the intimacy was implied.

"It's funny, who my mom thinks you are to me," Sabine said.

"Who's that?" Michael asked.

"I don't know yet," Sabine said. "I don't know if she is right or not."

His hug felt good, but she wasn't sure if it felt correct.

*

In the morning, when Sabine woke, her mother and Michael were already on their second cup of coffee, joking in the kitchen. Her mother was making waffles, and Michael was whipping cream.

"You're making him do it by hand?" Sabine asked, raising an eyebrow.

"Oh, you know, honey, you know I think it's better that way. Fluffier."

Michael had driven her close to a hundred miles, if she counted their first jaunt north, to get to her mother's home. He had slept on the sofa, and now he was whipping cream for their waffles with an old whisk and palling around. Sabine could see how her mother was ready to choose him, and Sabine could see that if it was a choice between her ex, who she couldn't even name—Sebastian? Ryan? SRyan?—and Michael, she'd choose Michael too.

The way the steam rose from the waffle iron seemed inexplicably hopeful. It seemed like the way smokestacks puffing smoke once felt like progress. It seemed like a curl of mist rising from a thawing pond. It seemed like a finger of cloud she could float on, like one of her birds in one of her bird-scapes.

The waffles were piled onto plates, the whipped cream into a bowl. Sabine's mother microwaved syrup, and the three of them layered it all on, sprinkling even more sugar on out-of-season strawberries. It was a gift, this meal.

Still, by the lunchtime dishes, Sabine pushed Michael out the door.

"How are you getting home?" he asked.

"I am home," she said.

She looked at her mother and looked at the kitchen, messy from cooking but bright, and Sabine wondered if there was a fortune for what she was feeling, something like *Why did you rush to leave the house of your family* or *You can return to the past if you try*, but mostly she could not go back to the apartment; she could not bend to pick up Ryan/ Sebastian from the floor or the sofa or wherever he had slept. She was sure he would have found their bed too dark and damp, and while she understood this, she could not take care of him. Would not take care of him.

Michael crossed the lawn to his car, and for a moment, Sabine wanted to go with him. He had been so kind to her, and now he was going to his own home, with his dad and his mom.

They were like moons, orbiting different planets.

I only need a few weeks, she whispered, not loud enough for him to hear. *Michael*.

Inside, her mother was doing dishes.

"He seemed nice," her mother said. "I certainly had fun with you two."

"I'm glad," Sabine said, though she didn't think any of it was about fun.

"Invite him over again, Beenie Girl," her mother said. "Nice-looking kid, too, if you want my opinion."

Sabine chatted some more with her mother, talking through how to handle the apartment, working out how long it would be okay to stay, and then Sabine went for a walk.

Almost unconsciously, she scoured the ground for feathers, even though she didn't think she really wanted to return to the bird-scapes. She had mostly liked the light quality of the presentation of her work, even though the actual canvases were quite heavy. Her mother said she could stay as long as she wanted. Her mother said to give the property management company proper notice, pay whatever she owed, and then to let SRyan get evicted if he couldn't take it from there. To take care of herself and not worry about him. Her mother said that when she'd left Sabine's father, she had thought she would never care for a man again, even though her friends who had been divorced said that would fade. Yet, of all the things she'd been wrong about in her life, her mother said, she had turned out to be right about love.

THE CENTER OF THE CIRCLE

In the commune where I had grown up, left, and then returned to, The Circle, my co-inhabitants complained about the way things were changing; they complained about our nation's political climate, they complained about the planting seasons being so much less predictable than years past, and they complained about the mice that were slinking through the outhouses, through the gardens. There had been a few years without a good killing freeze, so critters were abundant. I didn't like the mice either, but the complaining, it just wore me out.

*

The entire autumn after I'd come back to The Circle from Denver after losing my office job—the job that had seemed liked such a betrayal to my parents, to my community, but that suited me nonetheless—I slept in Jay's school bus house. We didn't always share the bed. That season, he was in love with me and I was in love with him, but I needed space, so sometimes I curled up in the softness of the old sofa pushed against the windows. He disliked it when I didn't default to him like I had when we were children, when we used to squeeze our bodies into a single sleeping bag in the grass. I had never planned on returning to his place, so some kind of permanence with Jay had never even crossed my mind, and I didn't want to stay with my parents.

How could I tell him that finding one another in adulthood was so unexpected? How could I tell him I didn't expect it to last?

*

I'm not sure what I wanted out of my homecoming, but it was harder than I had thought it would be. I saw how much older my parents were, how despite the organic food and the crystal-clear water of a mountain town, the sun exposure and subsistence work and financial stress had aged them.

I had known there wouldn't be space for my things, my city things, which was why I'd left most of them behind in Denver, but I also didn't know how firmly my family and the larger community had closed around the space I'd left open. Most of America expects their children will go out into the world, but I had been expected to stay, and I didn't realize how much of a wound I'd left, how thick the scar was.

Like everyone else, I filled my days working the property, and I signed up for the hardest jobs. My hours had been mostly screen time in Denver, typing away at the spreadsheets that filled my monitor. I wasn't sure if I had wanted to prove that the city hadn't made me soft or if I thought I needed to do this to show commitment, but I learned the city had ultimately made me soft. There were some nights that while I wanted Jay, my body was too sore to comply. Even when I felt the slick of heat between my legs, I'd sink into his sofa crammed into the school bus, up against the row of passenger side windows, and I'd fall asleep.

Mornings, the stickiness was still there, but Jay was already up, off to some chore, and I needed something stronger than herbal tea to get me through the morning.

He said I could sleep in the bed even if we weren't going to make love, but I hated that expression, *make love*, and I couldn't really sleep with him next to me anyway, and the couch was fine. The couch helped me at least pretend to keep a little distance.

One of the jobs I volunteered for was digging a new pit for an outhouse. I made a perfect square eight feet deep. I brought a small ladder with me into the pit, and a five-gallon bucket. When the bucket was full, I climbed the ladder and walked the dirt near one of the compost piles in the gardens. The wet earth smell was strong. It could have been millions of years since it had seen sun. As I got deeper in the hole, I'd stopped seeing even earthworms, and the soil felt desolate, perfect to piss on.

My entire body ached from the digging and from being up and down on the ladder with the bucket, fifty pounds of dirt straining my arm, switching the bucket to the other arm halfway up the ladder. I had more than enough cash from my savings to rent a small digging machine, which would have made the project last a day, but I didn't. Once the excavation was finally done, I bored a hole in the side of the main dirt wall and fitted it with pipe for a vent for the pit. I had hated the dull shovel, and I hated trying to tunnel through the dirt with a hand-cranked auger for the vent. I also hated trying to ram the pipe through the passage I'd made, but I finished it.

I wondered what I was doing, back in this place.

Jay helped me move the frame of an overflowing outhouse to the new site, and while he secured the frame to the ground, I filled in the old outhouse hole, with layers of ash from our woodstoves to help with decomposition, layers of dirt from the new hole. I sprinkled columbine seeds on top. I was sweaty and tired and smelling dirt and shit, and tired of smelling like dirt and shit.

*

What was this return, I wondered. The community hadn't asked me; I'd been dismissed from my job in the city and I had decided to go to where I thought home was. I thought they would welcome me. I suppose they did, in their way.

*

My parents lived in one of the few wood-framed houses in The Circle, one of the earliest dwellings, and their tenure in the community had earned them access to luxuries: the telephone that was always on the fritz and shared with many others; doors that closed; their own kitchen, even though they were generous about sharing it; they also had a deep freeze that was a serious draw on the solar electricity, but no one complained because my folks never complained if something was missing from the deep freeze, not that they would have used a word like *missing*. They weren't so old, but they were elders now.

They'd come to The Circle before they turned twenty, seeking a different life. They'd both come up around Chicagoland, but didn't meet until the same pickup truck scooped them up, my mom just before Davenport, Iowa, and my dad just outside of it. From there they had another five hours in the bed of a rattling Ford until they were dropped off in Omaha, and by that time their meeting had started to seem more like destiny—what were the chances, they had told me, that two kids both on their way west were offered a ride by the same guy along I-80. I didn't say I thought the chances were actually pretty strong, with so much rural road and really only one direct way to keep going. It was easier for my dad to get a ride with a woman, and it was less terrifying for my mother to accept one with a man.

It was summer. They'd both dropped out of college, and neither had a definite plan of where they would stop; they were both just heading to rough ideas picked from a map, into the wide expanse of sky, toward the mountains; my mom thought she might try for the West Coast, but the Rockies jutting up off of the plains had stopped her, just as they had stopped many travelers.

In Colorado they were seeing how the summer storms had soaked the foothills, and they saw how the hillsides were turning a violent green.

It was in the first weeks, with dripping trees bisected by patches of prickly pear, when they were dropped off on a side road, making their way toward the community they had heard about, that my mother understood she was pregnant. Another half day and they found the place that would become their home. In the first minutes, to hear them tell it, they were surrounded by bounty—they were fed herb salads from the garden, Palisade peaches, smoked venison. They were given clean bedding after bathing in the cold spring. The ladies wondered aloud if my mother might be with child, because her breasts were so plump on her slight frame. She was surprised the women were so attuned to her body already, before she could even remember all of their names. She nodded to them. They were right.

Then they washed and braided her hair, made her a crown of flowers, put their hands on her heart and her belly. They folded her in.

Still, this joy did not stop them from later cooking a tea, when my mother had missed her second moon and she had confided, to Barb-Ann first, and then to the group, that she wasn't ready to be a mother. She wasn't even close to ready.

Then she chugged pennyroyal laced with parsley and oranges that the women brought to her. The older ladies in the communities had brewed this concoction before, many times, but with my mom, it didn't stick. It wasn't a secret she'd tried to abort me, and she had told me not out of malice or sadness, but as a warning: *There are so many chemicals in our bodies now, the old herbs don't work as well. You need to know, for your own health.*

The women tipped their cups to my mother's lips, as many hands on the vessel as possible, making light of heavy work, doing their best—

with so many fingers on a teacup or a mason jar—to have no one person be responsible.

They kept this up until my mother missed her third period; the pregnancy was stuck and continuing to try and dislodge it would be dangerous. And this still did not stop them, even though their teas had had no effect, from switching to bringing my mother lentil soup and beef broth; it did not stop them from caring for her. From avoiding my father's advances, because even though they all, including my parents, believed in freedom from monogamy, and even if they might have desired him, a fresh body in their small community, they knew it was too much for their new sister. They cared for her from a place of complete acceptance, willing to both try to make an unplanned pregnancy go away and to welcome a new baby with handmade blankets. It wasn't that she didn't want me. She had longed to be a mother, but she was young and in a new place with my father. The women fashioned another crown for her to wear at my birth. I came into the world surrounded by these women, my mewling head scrambling to her breast. It was a day after her twentieth birthday.

These same women bared their own breasts if I was fussy and my mother tired; some of them had their own children and milk to spare, and some of them had been dry for years. In either case, they knew the comforts of the physical body and did not hold back.

That's how you know people love you, my mother said to me, when I told her I was leaving The Circle and she had told me again the story of her own arrival. *They do their best for you whether you are right or wrong, and whether they agree or not.*

Not many of the first women my mother had met in The Circle remained, except for Barb-Ann. Some had scattered to other communities, some had passed over, a few had given up on the hard winters and living close to animals and resettled in Denver. At least one woman had moved to Seattle, reconnecting with the child she had given up for adoption. I only knew this because there was a postcard of the Space Needle taped to the deep freeze, and once I

had peeled it off and read the backside. *She seems to have forgiven me, &
I live with her now. Husband is nice. Adopted parents are kind. Unexpected, to
reconnect w/ Watershine after years, tho they call her Sonja. (Their name. I like
mine better.) Miss you all, but I miss the time I could have had with my daughter
more. Trying to make up for it, be well & One Love.*

*

I wondered what kind of resolve I could have with Jay. I wasn't relying
on herbs to avoid pregnancy. I had a modern IUD with another three
years left on it. As much as they all fretted on chemicals, I couldn't
imagine any of the women, my mother included, would ever chide me
for using birth control, after their generation had fought for it. I knew
that now it was impossible for my mother to imagine how she would feel
if the teas and herbs had worked, but I also knew she had never gotten
pregnant again, and as a teenager, with Jay, I used to steal condoms
from her dresser drawer, even though if I had just asked, I am sure she
would have given them to me.

Still, I wondered how Jay's face might brighten, and I wondered
how my mother might take on a new energy, if I decided to open myself
to a pregnancy. I wondered if I owed it to them.

*

Jay was coming back from the sauna, heat shimmering off him in
waves, dripping condensation in the cool air, a small crocheted afghan
wrapped like a towel. I met him on the path to the new outhouse that
I had dug with my own hands, bundled in a mothy sweater and a pair
of his too-large boots. My feet were loose between the old leather and
pitted soles. I could tell he didn't expect to meet me.

"Melissa," he said. "You look cold."

"I am cold," I said.

"I'll build a fire in the bus," he said.

He didn't wait for my response, just turned, picking his way barefoot toward the only home he had ever known.

I pulled my pants down in the outhouse, and felt satisfied at how far my water had to fall. I hoped it would be a long time before I had to dig another hole like this.

*

As children in our home study, we'd learned that corporations and banks were only interested in profit, and that profit came at the expense of humans, other animals, and the land we lived on. This belief was not held by only us, Circle people, but also by other communities who opted for simplicity and a life lived close to our Mother Earth. We didn't think we were privileged. Then, I had felt the thrum of the earth's core. I had felt vibration of plants against soil. I had felt the pollen of flowers fall like dust motes. I had felt like the delicate balance of humans and other animals was a safe, if tenuous, negotiation. It seemed like work, with the bucket of dirt banging at my legs as I ascended a ladder out of the outhouse hole, and it seemed like very hard work with the continuous chopping of wood for cooking and heating, the constant scramble to grow and preserve food. The only cash economy was linked to the marijuana operations that dotted the forests and relied on Circle people to process and trim. I'd worked in one of these trimming trailers as a girl, motorhomes and camping outfits where we sat around the table and worked the flowers, the valuable part of pot, into saleable buds. There was plenty to barter, but sometimes we had needed real money. Herb salves cannot knit a broken bone. How much homemade jam would it have taken to pay a lawyer to settle a dispute after we'd diverted the creek and the adjacent landowner sued us for water rights. Someone must have had enough money, from something.

I didn't know what Jay thought about this. It was something no one really talked about, the pot money and how The Circle's gardening skills were attractive to growers. Colorado had moved toward legalization, but we were not part of the permitted scene. Too much government there for us, even if almost all of us were registered voters.

*

When I had first left, hitchhiking to Denver, it was because I had wanted something different. Then, I had my fall weed money, and I'd rented a small studio apartment and had shaved my dreads, my pits, my crotch, my legs.

For a while, I slept on the floor of my apartment in my sleeping bag, and then I got a mattress, though it was still on the floor for years. I kept my sheets clean, and I had gotten there myself. The solitude and the slip of my body between the folds of new fabric continued to feel emboldening even as the sheets thinned in the wash.

*

Whenever I was sleeping on the sofa in Jay's school bus, he would come to me.

"Are you staying," he would want to know.

"I'm not sure," I would say.

*

The night I saw Jay on the outhouse path and then followed him back to the bus, I was not too tired to fuck him. I fucked him with abandon. I knew I would be sore in every place in the morning, but I didn't care. We'd loved each other as children, and we loved each other now. His body against mine. His body inside mine. His body tethered to mine. What was the point of any of life's pain, if not this.

*

Still, no matter what nostalgia I had for The Circle, even the glow of Jay's body was not enough to smooth the rough places.

I hadn't really thought of her in years, but one day I was walking through the buildings and outbuildings, looking for something to do, and I remembered Claire. In Denver, I'd used my health insurance to get caught up on my vaccinations, and I always thought of Claire then, when the needle pierced my skin. She'd died when we were children, from chicken pox, or at least that's what we were told. Maybe she'd died from something more sinister and perhaps even something less. I wondered about measles or mumps or rubella. Either way, Claire, unvaccinated like all of the rest of us, had gotten very ill, and instead of being taken to a hospital, she'd been thrown her last birthday party.

I wanted to ask both of my parents about Claire, and I wanted to ask Jay what he remembered, since he'd known her too, but Claire was even more taboo than talking about how marijuana linked us to capitalism. Even in a community that had come up in the era of consciousness raising and rejection of systems and who was decidedly pro the raising of collective voices, the few times I spoke of Claire sparked something animal, something angry. To say her name was to question something that was much more than just an admission of failure.

In service of their own politics, they'd allowed a child to die.

If I had been an adult when Claire died, I'd also want to bury any thoughts about failing her deeper than even the outhouse hole, already deeper than a grave.

*

In Denver, first I had worked in a natural foods store that tolerated my transition to urbanism, and then I had transitioned to an office job where I looked at spreadsheets and sometimes wore pantyhose. *Tights* is what my mother would have called my stockings. It didn't matter.

Half a decade I was there, in the same studio apartment, and no one from The Circle ever came to see me. I had thought I might get a visitor or two who needed to crash on the way to a free clinic or on some errand, but I might have been just as off-limits as Claire. I would have opened my home to them. I would have made sure they had the kind of food they were used to, because I still ate that way, homemade yogurt and sprouted grains, avoiding pasteurization whenever I could, and always emphasizing plants over animals. There was kefir in my fridge, castile soap in my shower. Maybe I would have even put the razors away. Yet, no one came. Not my parents, not Jay, and not even someone passing through.

*

In the morning, I went to my parents' house in The Circle, wanting more privacy than the communal shower. They used the outhouses like everyone else—water was too precious to crap in, they believed, and also, why would you want to shit in your own home, my father said— but they did have a small tub, and they did have an on-demand hot-water heater that my mother said was really for the kitchen, but I knew she indulged in a bath now and again.

In my pack I still had a razor, which I hadn't touched since I'd returned, all the better that it would still be sharp.

I ran a sink full of hot water and, since there was no shaving cream, lathered up with shampoo. I took my curls off in chunks, gripping the hair close the scalp and cutting it clean. When I'd taken off my dreads, I had saved them, but the loose strands now were too chaotic to save, so I put the foamy locks in the garbage bin to keep from clogging the drain.

It was hard to tell if there was a breeze in the room or if it was just the new pink of my scalp, and I didn't stop. I cleaned my armpits, my legs, and my sex of hair. I scraped my forearms, my eyebrows.

Rinsing in the tub, the already hot water felt hotter after scraping my skin with the blade. I remembered this from before. I wished I had clean clothes to put on, but I did not, and so I wrapped in a thin towel and hurried back to Jay's school bus. I didn't expect to find him at home, but there he was, brewing tea and smoking a joint.

"Melissa," he said. "You're bare."

"I am." I realized I had accidentally left the razor in the bathroom, and my stomach turned knowing that my parents would see the disposable handle. They'd say I knew better than to incorporate single-use plastic items into my life, and they'd be right. My dirty clothes were left behind too, but they wouldn't care about them.

Already, I felt bumps forming where I'd pushed too hard, or where the skin was thin. My kneecap. The nape of my neck. Already, I felt incomplete knowing there were places that might not have been done completely. The middle of my back. My asshole. The regret of this I did not remember when I'd shaved myself before.

"I have a comfrey tincture that I can stretch with olive oil," Jay said, noticing that some of my skin was red.

He took a clean sheet from the storage under the bench seat and spread it across the floor. He rubbed me from head to toe and back, and he anointed me even in places the razor had not grazed. My nipples. My ears. The bottoms of my feet. My clit.

"Can you stay with me here, Melissa?" he asked, working more oil in. It felt good, smooth. My towel was long discarded, and somewhere between my calves and the undersides of my arms, Jay had become naked too. I was on my back and his cock was hard and he'd moved one hand to touch himself, while he kept the other on me, thumb working at my center, two fingers inside.

I couldn't help but think what a mess the sheet would be to wash, how hard we'd have to scrub to get it clean. How we'd find patches of gloss on the floor for days. Then the way he started moving in me made me think I could actually stay with him and do so with honesty, made me forget about the soiled sheet, made me forget about my hair, made me forget about how I'd gotten here, made me think this, this, this, only this.

*

The world with Jay shifted some. I stayed on the sofa, mostly, but I met him on the floor more and more often, and there was a part of that which made sense to me, to feel the unforgiving tile of the school bus at my back or on my knees. How I found bruises on my elbows and wrists, even though Jay was gentle, always gentle, when we were *making love*. I still hated the expression, even though I felt a deepening of my feelings toward Jay.

Just before the weather turned to deep winter, we had one of those Colorado days where the sun was out and the light was golden and it felt like snow could never come, while everything gleamed and we sweated through our undershirts.

Most of the fall work was done, and Barb-Ann organized a cookout in the communal kitchen—it was potluck and the remainders of the autumn crop, like squash that were not quite good enough to store but still good enough to eat, items that had to be cleared from the deep freeze, and potatoes with shovel scars. We cleaned and ate our leftovers and ugly produce; we found guitars and banjos and drums. Someone donated homemade wine that was not particularly tasty, but was certainly potent, and we danced until the moon began to peek over the trees.

By the next evening, a storm front would come in, and we'd enter a brutal cold that would freeze a few chickens who hadn't gotten to shelter and make going to the outhouse miserable and sometimes impossible. In the beginning, the wind would come so hard I worried the school bus would tip, and Jay and I would sit on the side that was taking impact, to add weight.

I would have to decide then, as the old windows creaked and the gusts felt as if they could lift the tires, if I could stay in this life with Jay. He would have to decide if he would have me, though I think he was already sure.

"Has it ever blown over?" I asked him. I felt like I would have remembered something like this, but I wasn't positive.

"It's pretty solid," he said. "And the frame is anchored to the ground, though it has been awhile since I checked the cables."

I didn't point out that he hadn't answered my question. We were in the center of the circle, where Jay's folks had parked the bus three decades ago, and it hadn't moved since. The tires were long gone and the engine parted out; it rested on concrete blocks, and someone had woven yarn through the steering wheel to make it look like a dreamcatcher. It looked like a child's work. As Jay pulled me closer, and we leaned toward the direction of the wind, I wondered if it might have been mine.

THE HUMAN

On the night before Michael's stepfather, Dave, was taken to the skilled nursing facility, he felt sure this was not the way it should work. Dave was dying, but everyone was dying. So much had changed in even Michael's own lifetime, he couldn't imagine how Dave was feeling, and Michael was feeling mortality more than he ever had, since he'd turned fifty.

Medical technology had continued to advance, and particularly in the early '20s, there was a sense of incredible hope. Michael had been young then and hadn't cared so much about age reversing processes or cures for arthritis, but he certainly cared now.

Seeing Dave being carted off to the old-age home, Michael wondered what had gone so wrong. The year Dave had been born, 1959, man still had a decade before landing on the moon. In 2031, when Dave was seventy-two and Michael was thirty-six, an international consortium had established a moon colony. It had seemed like science fiction when morning daytime TV did human interest segments on the colonists, and it seemed like science fiction when the government started looking for volunteers—debt and student loan forgiveness were some of the perks. Life insurance for family left behind of course, and the legacy of a living among the stars.

Even when the civilian recruitments first started, Michael was not interested. The earliest moon colonists had been retired or washed out American astronauts, Russian cosmonauts, and Chinese taikonauts, a pool which was exhausted fairly quickly. Many of the people who had been in orbit did not want to go back, and the ones in space programs who had not made the cut in earlier years were either bitter or had moved on.

The next round of recruits were military. And then civil servants, returning Peace Corps volunteers. Postal workers and city council members, teachers.

There was talk of a draft, but the idea did not test well, so nations moved to public relations campaigns.

In America, whenever the colony was on the news, the hotline to call or text or video chat flashed at the end of the segment.

Michael was happy for the colonists. They seemed to have a nice life, earning their government salaries and growing vegetables under a geodesic dome. In one human interest piece, the colonists showed a typical meal, sourced from their vertical, hydroponic gardens. It featured kale and herbs. Texturized protein powder, developed by NASA and delivered in compressed bricks, was sprinkled liberally over the colonist's salads.

"Our food is really good," a woman with a southern American accent said. She was young and pretty, long eyelashes, pink cheeks. "We have a closed loop system so all of our waste goes back to the garden, but sterilized. And I'm learning Mandarin! *Nǐ hǎo!*" she waved.

The protein powder was also available in American supermarkets, and Michael didn't know if was a product that had gained popularity because of placement in space, like Tang, or if it was being placed in life to get people used to it.

In any case, occasionally when he went out, he'd see it on the menu of upscale restaurants, alongside microgreens and artisan cheese. Protein powder pops, soaked in tamari and served on a skewer. Deep fried protein powder strips served with "astronaut aioli," whatever that was, tasted like someone had combined Miracle and Cool Whip. His least favorite was when the protein powder appeared in a shaker, along with salt and oil as if it were some fundamental part of culinary history.

He did understand the push to the moon and why it was necessary. Even developed countries had been on meat rations for years. Cattle, first, and then swine, and later fowl and fish were designated as a drain on resources and could not be commercially farmed. Dairies and feedlots transitioned to soy and hemp. At first, at least in America, people who lived outside of urban centers were living better than city folks, with their gardens and livestock. Increasingly, it was the rural who were becoming wealthy, selling steaks and lamb shanks to what was left of the urban rich. He'd read an article about how billionaires would helicopter to remote farms and islands to pick up tenderloin and oysters, though eventually even the helipads were converted into cultivation spaces.

Even alternative proteins like tofu and tempeh were getting expensive for ordinary people, and his yard, just like the yards of everyone he knew, had transitioned away from passive lawn to active production. Personally, he agonized over the chickens. He had studied communication and business, so at first he had no idea what to do with the flock of chicks he'd gotten at the community center, but they grew, and then he tried to balance filching eggs from his hens' clutch with ensuring they would propagate. There was an incredible amount of literature on backyard animal husbandry online, and he devoted himself to learning.

Currently, the birds were okay. New chicks had hatched, he'd butchered some of the grown hens, which was awful, but he had his own little corner of abundance. He fed the birds, and their shit fed his garden, and their eggs appeared like fragile gifts. Still, the hens seemed to be always molting and they were cranky, always hot. He related. The one rooster strutted like a king, and Michael hated him. In the perpetual heat, he'd hung a fan in the coop, and he put out old, freezer burnt frozen vegetables when temperatures soared into the hundreds. The chickens did not seem to care that a block of peas was half a decade old, but even Michael's deepest freezer stores were becoming depleted, because no one shopped the way they used to. Nothing ever went on sale.

Many cities were very organized, with rooftops converted and common areas commandeered. His suburb outside of Denver had not yet enacted any strict official ordinances, but Michael let the chickens peck what was left of his grass into nothing anyway, and he fenced in his vegetable garden to keep them away from the squash. When he had produce that was stunted or immature, he sliced it and put it in ice trays with water, and then turned out the cubes into plastic bags to make room for more. He did this not only for the chickens but for the future.

*

Michael's mother had died the year of the moon push. Unexpectedly, and immediately he had started to get letters and phone calls from the government, identifying him as a strong candidate for the colony.

When he spoke with a representative by phone, she said, "Now that both of your parents are gone, you might want to consider it, for the greater good. Tell me, what's keeping you on Earth?"

Michael had long known that as an unmarried man, he'd be a target for moon life. He had not expected it to come on so quickly.

He also realized the caller had more information than he had about his own biological father. It didn't affect him emotionally, but he hadn't known his birth father was dead.

"You know, my actual dad is still alive," he said. "His name is Dave."

"Your *step*father, you mean, is David, and yes, living, according to our records, in the 2000 block of Marion Street, Denver, Colorado."

"And I have a sister," Michael said. "And I don't want to go to the moon. Can you take me off this list?"

"Your *step*sister, you mean, Leah, according to our records. We do not have her address on file. I don't have the authority to remove you from any list, but I can add Leah, if you'd rather go together. She has some problems, though, I see in the notes. Would you like to provide an update on Leah's current legal residence? This will help us make contact."

Michael hung up.

His phone rang again and he sent it to voicemail.

His phone rang every hour, on the hour, from the same number, for the next seventy-two hours. When it stopped, he knew he had only been temporarily cycled out.

*

They'd waited for months for the approval from insurance regarding Dave's placement to the nursing home to come through. Man was living on the moon but Medicare was still a disaster. When his mother had been diagnosed with pancreatic cancer, Medicare had transitioned immediately to palliative.

Michael knew there was an algorithm, and he knew that his mother did not have a good chance of survival—some things never changed, he figured—but he was surprised at how quickly the system dismissed her.

"Would it hurt to try to treat it?" he had asked the administrator. "I've seen the ads for Pancrestia, or I could probably talk her into a trial of something experimental."

"It won't help," the administrator had said. "Late stage, you know, most of the developments are in detection."

Maybe he was not surprised.

He missed his mother, but he was glad she was gone. On her deathbed, she had expressed great concern for him and his sister. She had begged him not to have her body cremated, but Michael had cremated his mother anyway. He couldn't afford a cemetery—land was too precious and prices had soared—and he didn't want her composting in his backyard, though it was one of the options in the pamphlets provided by hospice. He was glad she did not have to see how all this moon business had escalated.

He had been unable to imagine loading the car and driving Dave the few miles to his new room at St. Peter Home, but when it was happening, he went through the motions.

They were not a religious family, but Michael liked that Saint Peter had ultimately become a saint by performing miracles of compassion. At least according to Wikipedia.

Illness had come very quickly after his mother and Dave had come back from vacation in Mexico. They had thought there was something lingering from the water, but Michael reminded them they'd stayed in a resort and also, he had said then, there were 145 million people in Mexico—the water couldn't be that bad. Maybe it gave you the shits if you weren't used to it, but it didn't keep you in bed for three days.

Then his mother collapsed.

Dave was lucid enough to call 911, just barely, but it made no difference.

Michael was aware of the rumors, though he thought the stories about poisoning were the same hysteria of 1960s America when people thought LSD was in the municipal supplies. The border between the US and Mexico had been re-opened in 2024 after the wall had come down and it certainly hadn't solved everything, but it seemed reasonable enough to go to Mexico for vacation. The tourism brochures were so glossy.

He also didn't think that whatever had killed his mother and had made Dave very sick, sick in an unrecoverable way, was something Mexico had done.

How many other able-bodied men and women were getting calls about the moon colony, after their folks succumbed to a resort poisoning, he wondered. He didn't dare look it up to be recorded in his browser history. He was so sorry he'd been so naïve. He'd taken them to the airport. He'd been proud of them for traveling on their own.

What the fuck, he thought.

*

Michael called his sister Leah.

"It would be good if you could come here," Michael said to his sister. "Dave would like to see you. I can get you a ticket."

"Yeah, I dunno Mikey. Work is pretty busy."

Leah was living in Honolulu, and he honestly was not sure what she did for a living. She had flown back briefly for their mother's funeral, staying in her childhood bedroom and alternating between rage and desperate sadness. Michael knew which it was by the music she listened to.

Whenever Michael asked his sister about her work, she demurred. "Employment here is not like the mainland, brother," but that didn't tell him anything. She was old enough, forty, that he didn't think she was still dancing—she had sworn him to secrecy about it years ago and he had kept that promise—but he worried now that she was still doing some kind of sex work.

And he didn't care if she was, as long as she was safe, as long as she was stable. He remembered when she was born. He remembered helping her with her homework. He remembered when he was thirty-one and she'd just turned twenty-one the call he'd gotten from her, slurry drunk and angry, out at a club, begging him to come pick her up. She was still in Denver then, but he was out of town on a business trip, so he'd found a friend to go for her. She was not coherent enough to give her address, and Michael didn't know it, because she was shuffling through different houses all the time. His friend, Laird, was a guy he had worked with at the office with Dave, and Laird was solid. The kind of guy who didn't ask a lot of questions when you called after midnight with a favor even though you hadn't really talked in over a year, the kind of guy who upon realizing Leah didn't know where her own home was took her to his, set her up on his inflatable mattress, made her eat a sandwich and drink a glass of water, who texted Michael later to say *I'm so sorry, but when I woke up she was gone.*

*

The woman who was the moon representative started dialing him again. Every hour, on the hour. He had turned his phone to silent, and then powered it all the way down, but somehow it still lit up and rang.

In the television segments, moon life was increasingly rosy. The first child had been born, a Russian girl with dark hair. They called her Луна, Yuèliàng, and Luna. The media agreed she was beautiful, and even Michael felt a kind of closeness with the space baby, and so he answered his phone at midnight on a Tuesday in a wash of remembering his sister being born.

"Michael," the representative said, "You have work tomorrow; you can't really talk now, you know."

"Did you call to tell me this?" he asked.

"Let's make an appointment for tomorrow at 10 a.m., your time. Your calendar looks free," she said.

"Fine," he said.

"Are you sad you never had children?" she asked, "Remember your ex-girlfriend from those years ago, Sabine? She has two, but she's divorced now."

"You're right. I need to go back to sleep," he said.

"Here we don't sleep," the representative said, "And we are very happy."

"I don't believe you," Michael said, but the representative had already hung up.

*

At the facility, Dave was settling in. The doctors said he had Rapid Advance Parkinson's (RAP), a new kind, and Michael wasn't sure if this was true, but if it was, it was terrifying, and for the first time in his life, he was glad to not share Dave's genes.

He called his sister again, but she didn't pick up. *Listen, Lee, like I said, I will buy your ticket. Please come. I can't do this on my own.*

She texted back almost immediately. *It's not about money, Mikey. Why do you always think that? You are just like him!*

That's a compliment, you know, sis, he tapped.

Fuck off, Mike.

Love you too.

He hated texting, and he wondered what Dave had ever done to Leah, besides care for her. It was easy to be angry at his sister, now that Dave was dying.

At home, after work, Michael heard a thumping sound at his front door, and when he opened it, there was a package, tied in string.

Inside, several blocks of protein powder sealed in a biodegradable film, a braid of fat garlic—his had wilted this year, and he wasn't sure why—and sealed inside dry ice, one very fresh looking beefsteak. He hadn't had beef in probably half a decade.

Just as he was putting the beef onto his barbeque, which he'd had to dig out of storage and then try and find enough wood scraps to burn in it, his phone rang with the inscrutable digits of a representative on the caller ID, but he didn't answer.

*

There was a whisper about diseases, early onset Alzheimer's, abrupt and acute RAP, and cancers that had been accepted as incurable, like pancreatic, like Michael's mother had had. Especially in people who were non-compliant. Or so the whispers said. There were some exclusively print journals that printed theories and leafleted the city streets. Lymphomic episodes were a hot topic.

Michael was getting bolder about checking internet message boards, and though he had always been a reserved person, he did think there was some weight to what people were saying—*we cured the AIDS virus and yet there's nothing for diseases that have been around longer?*

When he'd spoken to the representative at their appointed time on Wednesday, his ordinarily low level of alarm had peaked.

"Mikey, you have another year," she said. "Did you enjoy the steak?"

"What does that mean," he said. Only his family called him "Mikey." Now he was worried that he shouldn't have eaten the beef. He'd sprinkled one portion of the protein powder on the chicken feed, and he wondered if the representative somehow knew about that too.

"Also, Leah," she said. "Leah, we have been looking into it and we do not think she is going to become a moon candidate."

He wondered if he was actually speaking to an automated system. He had said to the representative that he wanted to stay on earth, didn't some humans have to stay? The moon was less than thirty percent of the size of Earth, with no water outside of the closed-loop domes. Even he knew that. Kids learned it in school. No way it could support large populations.

"We're about to begin terraforming," the representative said. "We think this will create change, and the potential on Mars especially is exciting."

Schoolkids also knew Mars was only half the size of Earth.

"What about Sabine," Michael said. He heard his chickens clucking.

"She's a candidate," the representative said. "You have an algorithmic match with her. You think of her. We know."

"I haven't talked to her in years," Michael said, backtracking. "I have never kept in touch with my exes."

"Does that matter now?" the representative asked, but before he could answer, the call disconnected.

*

The absolute worst thing, when Michael was strapped into the transport rocket's jump seat, was thinking about Dave. In the prior eleven months, dementia had escalated, and while Dave was not there on the surface, Michael believed Dave was in there somewhere. He had unsuccessfully lobbied to bring Dave to the moon based on shaky evidence that low gravity could be beneficial to neurological diseases.

There was a trial study, but the panel did not agree in Michael's favor, largely because Dave was unable to consent.

"As if you care so much about consent!" he had almost shouted at the hearing, but he held back.

He'd been fired from his job, his chickens had died all at once, overnight, and his vegetable garden turned to black mold. He thought he saw the outline of a footprint in the garden, but he couldn't be sure. His bank account was frozen. The hotline said it was just an administrative error and they would release money if he called them, but even in the small amounts they approved, the money was going fast, and he didn't think it was an error at all.

"I will take care of Dave," Michael had said as he argued to bring his stepfather, the only father he had known.

"It's better that he stays," the panel said. "Your sister can care for him."

"And if she can't? I haven't spoken to her. She won't return my calls. What happens then?"

"The facility does their job, and we are looking out," the panel of representatives said, in what seemed like unison.

The moon consortium had given final approval on matching him with Sabine. He'd asked for her out of the shortlist, or he had accepted the suggestion of her, as at least she was someone he knew, though it had been years since he'd seen her, and though he still had not spoken to her nor exchanged a message, she had accepted him too. He understood he would be going to the moon whether he wanted to or not.

He would become a father to her children, just like Dave had been a father to him. He would resolve to transcend the past, just as Dave had. He would watch the children grow. Just a few hours after he had landed, he would be shepherded to her pod, and the union between Michael and Sabine would be sealed in a government ceremony, a representative presiding.

"What if my shuttle is late," Michael had asked, worried about starting his nuptials incorrectly.

"Don't be so terrestrial," the representatives had said. "We are never late."

*

The dome Michael shared with Sabine was clean and spare. They realized they were luckier than some of the other matches, having some context on Earth.

"Your mother?" Michael asked on their wedding night, his first night in the colony. Sabine had been on-Moon for a month.

"She went fast," Sabine said. "Then the calls started."

"I know," Michael said.

"Remember when all I cared about was art?"

"Yes. I remember."

Sabine was divorced, and the father of her children had an exemption—he did something with chemicals, for the government, and he had remained on Earth. Sabine said that she had only married the man because she thought it would mean she could stay.

A girl and a boy with Sabine's fine features also occupied the dome. And it was not long before Sabine's belly grew with another girl who became another space baby.

"I didn't think I could still conceive," Sabine had whispered, "I had to do fertilization for the other kids. But I'm sure. I have to report it."

She punched her symptoms into the console in their living room.

The next day, a representative arrived, and tested Sabine's urine and blood. "Low gravity has this effect, it regenerates the body."

"I'm fifty-two," Sabine said. "I already did menopause."

"We will be monitoring you. Congratulations."

Michael felt a pang for Dave. He had a video call with him once a week, but Dave seemed not to register who he was.

"We're having a baby, Dad," Michael said.

"Oh, congratulations to Leah!" Dave said.

Michael had made regular inquiries about his sister Leah, but nothing had turned up. Hawaii had voted to secede from the United States, and he hoped it was just because of that—no information being shared, rather than no information to be had.

On the night of their child's birth, Michael gave to Sabine the package he had smuggled from Earth and had been saving, hidden in on tiny corner of his small closet, a soft bag of chicken feathers he'd collected once he knew he was matched with Sabine and as his birds died.

"You do remember me from then," she said. "I thought you might have been faking it. The bird-scapes. The art I made."

"Yes," he said, even though it was only half a memory, from another time.

*

For years, they lived in harmony. For years the children grew, and the youngest girl especially, moon-child, who did not look at Earth with nostalgia. When her siblings were depressed, she cheered them up. When her parents wondered what they were actually doing, she assured them. When the oxygen levels were low in the dome or the artificial gravity apparatus not functioning, she was animated, suspended from the ceiling, and certainly not conserving energy as the training literature suggested. Rather than being terrified, she laughed and pushed off of the wall for more momentum on her aerial somersault.

Their days were filled with working in the gardens, repairing the geodesic dome, repairing the closed loop water and waste systems, repairing the pods the community lived in, and filing requests to the representatives.

The representatives called back sometimes, inquiring about health and welfare.

"What's your location, actually?" Michael asked once.

"Be careful," the voice said.

The youngest girl they called Joy. They'd not bothered to learn the Russian and Mandarin pronunciations of her name, because the pods had splintered and intercultural training had ceased just before Joy was born. From Sabine's first marriage, the boy Jesu, was petulant and moody. The oldest girl, Corinne, was skeptical and bored. Michael and Sabine were sorry for their Earth kids. They hadn't asked for this.

They had friends from some of the other pods, but upon every orbit of the home planet, it became clearer and clearer they would never go back. The children themselves were no longer children. Jesu became nineteen and Corinne twenty-one. They would always have a guaranteed salary, as part of the colony, but there was little to engage with outside of manual labor and physical training for the always upcoming Mars expedition.

Michael remembered once when he'd been a child himself, and Dave, who was just a stranger then, had waited on his mother's stoop. Michael had handed water to Dave through the screen door, even as he'd felt bad about not inviting the older man in, but he was home alone and his mother had very strict instructions.

How nice it would be, Michael thought, to just go outside. How nice it would be to just breathe, and not wonder about the filtration system, not wonder where the next breath was coming from.

*

It happened slowly, fewer transports from Earth, fewer stopovers on the convoys to Mars. Moon colonists saw plenty of rockets, but the bays to their pods stayed empty, and stores were running low.

Michael had convinced the colonists to make some risky adjustments to the oxygen and the water systems, and his bet had paid off. The monitors were beeping less urgently, but they still needed supplies.

Even the protein powder, their staple, was becoming depleted.

Michael was the same age now that Dave had been when he had gone to the facility. He loved Sabine, but he wasn't sure if his life was better.

Those years ago, Sabine had brought her own contraband, starts of peace lily and mother-in-law tongue, high oxygen producers, and their dome was filled with leaves. She tried to give cuttings to their neighbors, but the neighbors disapproved.

The literature said to trust the system.

Sabine said she did trust the system, but just like on Earth, even though she trusted the grid, *or, eh, the system*, she said she put solar panels on her roof to supplement.

"The reps don't like us to talk about Earth," the neighbors said.

"It's not 'talking about Earth' to grow something," Sabine said.

Outside every window, Mars was looking different from terraforming, a kind of purple, and Earth was looking different, too, aquamarine.

Sabine said she thought the seas had risen and the cities had been consumed, and that's why no government was sending them relief.

"Don't say that so loud," Michael said.

"They hear it all anyway," she said. "We haven't heard from a representative in months. What does that tell you?"

The home planet was pretty, as she'd always been, but it was true there were fewer tufts of green or brown or white-capped mountains—where were the people living? They were not, mostly, they assumed.

*

And then the representatives arrived all at once, in smart uniforms with flush cheeks, looking healthy and well-fed.

They had transport vehicles. Mars was finally ready but there were limited seats.

"There will be enough for everyone eventually," the representative of the representatives said. "For now, it's just a matter of timing. There are still ejection capsules in the event of an emergency for those who remain."

Almost all of the parents sent their children on ahead. Michael and Sabine did. Joy, their moon baby, was for the first time in her life, scared. Jesu and Corinne, for the first time in their lives, were able to comfort her because they already knew what it was like to leave home.

When they said goodbye to the children, there was another few days left of oxygen remaining on the limping generator.

When they looked out the window of their dome, they were too far out of orbit to have any real information.

They saw, even though no one believed them, the aurora borealis.

They saw their children being carried away by rocket.

They saw the meter on the air filtration system tick to below critical levels.

They saw, thankfully after the children had gone, the last moments of hypoxia take hold of their friends and neighbors in a rapture of asphyxiation, tearing at corners of the dome, breaking bottles of contraband champagne against the trusses, lighting a bonfire of clothes and household goods. The small amount of NASA's remaining protein powder, tossed into the blaze, burned in an unconventional rainbow, chartreuse to mauve to gold.

Michael and Sabine saw the fires, knew the fires would feed on the little oxygen left. They wondered how much pressure it would take to cause the dome to explode.

Then Sabine was grabbing Michael's hand, running towards one of the escape capsules. It was confusing, that there were so many left, that so few colonists had decided to eject. ·

"We should have gone sooner," Michael said. "Why didn't we follow the kids directly?"

"It's the air. We haven't been thinking straight," Sabine said. "I should have had more plants. They were right to take the children. Dirt was so hard to get. And they mocked me, remember how they mocked me? The children are safe, though, that's what matters."

Sabine wept and Michael remembered what he'd learned long ago in a yoga class with Dave: breathe in, but remember to breathe out.

He exhaled, and eventually so did Sabine.

They had both been trained on aeronautical controls but the capsule had only a single button and so they pushed it together.

A thruster engaged, and they both felt the force. They hovered for a moment, and then they cried out: immediately it was clear they were on a trajectory towards Earth, not towards Mars. The launch codes were apparently old and so they hurtled towards what was once their homeland but was now a hot ocean.

Or the codes were not old.

"I thought we'd go the other way," Michael said.

"Me too," Sabine said.

"We'll burn up in the atmosphere," Michael said. "It will go fast."

"Maybe," Sabine said. "I'm not sure what these things are made of." She thumped the side of the capsule.

They felt clearer than they had in days, from the capsule's oxygen supply.

"What will the representatives tell our children," Michael said.

"He was a kind man, a kind father," Sabine said, breathing deeply.

"She was a gifted artist, a good mother," Michael said, exhaling.

"They made a family," she said.

"They were a family," he said.

They were two, hurtling towards a dead planet, fingers laced together, the ends of their gray hair starting to spark, glowing filaments in the first microseconds of re-entry.

Then their bodies were ash, and then their bodies were nothing, and what was left of the capsule splashed down, where it began to quickly dissolve in the acidity of the surrounding sea.

CHRISTIAN

NOT ME

It wasn't until my second affair that my first one really sunk in. I was on a bench under a tree in the park, waiting for my lover, Leah. Leah with the tangled hair, snags from crown to tip, lost bobby pins and barrettes woven in. Leah, always in a wrinkled tank dress looking like it was pulled from the laundry for just one more wear, Leah who borrowed money from me the last time I saw her and might have only be continuing to see me under the pretense of paying it back, which I was fine with.

Leah was a dancer, and she was barefoot on the grass as she tracked her way through the park to meet me, carrying her sandals.

I met her when she was dancing. I'd had too much champagne. Strip joints had never been part of my life, but when my cousin had moved back to Colorado from New Mexico, we'd reconnected, and clubs were what he liked to do. I hadn't known this about him, but it was fun. I wasn't much of a drinker anymore, but the champagne had that celebratory quality, so, why not, I figured.

The context was that a decade into my marriage to my wife Raquel, we'd mostly decided to live life apart, even if we still had our moments.

The first time I went to a club with my cousin, Raquel was at Burning Man. Why anyone over thirty would have any interest in Burning Man was beyond me, but Raquel said I was being uptight.

Then, Leah, on the stage, leaning towards me.

Leah, glowing perfectly ringed in feather and sequin and teased hair backlit from the spotlight.

My wife was out in the Nevada desert, probably half or fully naked and pumped full of acid or ecstasy or molly or drugs I hadn't even heard about.

So why not buy a lap dance from a beautiful girl. Why not fantasize that I could take her home.

My first affair had been a lot more pedestrian. I'd moved on from a job where I worked with my wife's cousin—I was the IT person and Raquel's cousin Lisa was CFO. That's how we'd met. More accurately, I was fired, and Lisa was still there. It was actually nice not to be on staff with Lisa anymore and just be family.

The first affair, though, was just me on a business trip, for training. At the job that was new at the time, they sent us to Chicago to get synced up with the central office and after the final work day was finished, we did a booze cruise on Lake Michigan.

I actually hadn't known how beautiful the Great Lakes were, and I thought of Raquel, who at one point in her life had made it a goal to visit all of the world's seas—and she'd gotten to many of them, sometimes with me, sometimes without. I thought then, while the freshwater lapped at the side of the chartered boat, to suggest to her that big lakes could be a next, new bucket list—Superior, Michigan, Huron, Ontario, Erie, the Salt Lake. Victoria and Tanganyika in Africa, Baikal and Ladoga in Russia, Lake Van in Turkey and Saimaa in Finland. Searching on my phone, I started making plans.

Raquel had introduced me to travel, but it had been a few years since we'd been on a trip together, and I was pleased at myself for thinking of this, the lakes. It could be an olive branch. It could make her happy.

On the fly, I created a Google doc and shared it with my wife, hoping that the electronic *ping* of my message would remind her that I did think of her, I did care for her, I did have some ideas about our future together, even if we had been recently struggling to connect. I populated the Google doc with as many ideas I could find in between conversations with coworkers and trips to the bathroom, but Raquel didn't respond, and I didn't see that she'd logged in and made any changes. I checked the permissions, yes, she was able to edit, and then I shared the link again this time over text, just in case it had gotten snagged in her email spam, but still she didn't reply.

A few hours later, with not a word from Raquel, the boat had long since docked and I was perched on a bar seat with a coworker who lived in Omaha, and then everyone else had gone back to their rooms, and then the coworker was in mine. I'll not pretend it was an accident: I invited the coworker to my room, and I did it because I was pissed at my wife for not replying to me, and I called and ordered two more beers from room service along with a piece of cheesecake, which we didn't eat. Halfway through fucking my coworker, I remembered that it was my wife Raquel who liked cheesecake, not me, and apparently not the slim Midwesterner between my sheets.

The next morning there were a string of texts on my phone and two missed calls from Raquel, a voicemail that said her cell had been on silent and she'd been watching a movie and then had fallen asleep. *Haha funny.* I tapped back. *Me too.*

*

Maybe I was feeling a bit confident when I thought I could get Leah's number, because my cousin said there was no way. My cousin said the only reason that his wife didn't flip about him going to strip clubs was that she felt like it as the same difference between going to a movie and watching a play—in person, at a play, maybe the actors felt closer, but they were still just as off limits and uninterested in the observers as actual cinema celebrities were.

Stupid sounding as it was, I wrote my cell on twenty bucks and tucked into Leah's bra strap the next time she came around.

"That's a tired move," my cousin said. "And really, twenty bucks? You're insulting her."

She called though.

"Because she thinks you're a sucker," my cousin said later.

He was probably right.

*

"Hey Chris," Leah said, sitting down on the park bench with me. No one called me Chris. I had always gone by my full name, Christian, but with Leah I didn't mind.

There was something very familiar in the center of her face— she looked like someone that I was sure I knew, but I couldn't place. I wondered if maybe she'd been an intern once, at my old office, but she never mentioned anything about her life before dancing.

"Don't you want to do something different?" I had asked her.

"Mind your own business," she said. "We aren't falling in love over here. And you sound like my brother and it's grossing me out."

"What's your brother do again?"

"Fuck off, Chris."

On the park bench, we chatted about our schedules for the day, and I asked Leah when her shift started, but she said she was off. I said I wished she would stop dancing. Not because of some moralistic position, but because I thought she was more intelligent than it.

"You don't know shit," she told me. "I don't have half the brains of most of the women who work in that place. We do it because we can make money, that's it. You are the dummies that pay us. One of the other gals and I are talking about moving to Hawaii. We won't need to pay for spray tan in the winter then because there is no winter. How's that for smart."

We left the park and walked to lunch. We both had burgers with no bun and a glass of pink wine. We went back to the home I shared with Raquel who was out of town again; I had had Leah over before so she went straight to the guestroom. A cold propriety, but maybe worth something, to refrain from defiling the marital bed.

"You're actually not even that attractive, Chris," she said to me, naked on the beige company sheets. "I know what I see in you, but I don't understand what your wife sees in you."

"What do you see in me?"

Leah rolled her eyes. "That you'd even ask makes me want to take it back," she said.

In the morning, I woke to her nuzzling against me. I'd been dozing for a few hours at most, but she seemed rested. The afternoon and into evening we had been in and out of the guestroom, ordered delivery ramen with low carb Shirataki noodles, padded around the house in our underwear, polished off some of Raquel's tequila which I made a mental note to replace with a bottle three-fifths of the way gone not a full one—she'd notice something amiss if there was wrapped, untouched bottle—and tried to work out a duet of *Leather and Lace*. Leah said Stevie Nicks was the kind of music her mother listened to, but I just liked the lines.

Lovers forever, Face to face
My city your mountains, Stay with me stay
I need you to love me, I need you today
Give to me you leather, take from me, my lace

"You're such a dork, Chris," Leah said, through the chorus.

"*You in the moonlight, with your sleepy eyes*," I sang the male part badly, but with emotion. I was feeling it. "*Could you ever love a man like me?*"

Leah lurched for my phone which was connected to the Bluetooth speaker.

"I think I told you before, we aren't falling in love," she said, stabbing at the app and halting the song.

Then I tried to tell her it was just the moment. Then I tried to tell her I was only trying to have fun. Then I tried to tell her I was worried she would really move to Hawaii and I would never see her again. Sputtering, drunk off Raquel's tequila, I tried to ask Leah if it was really so bad if I loved her.

"Seriously, Chris?" she said. "You are such an idiot."

*

This wasn't the Burning Man weekend, it was just a different time when Raquel was gone, and not due back until late afternoon, but I had a sudden panic when I woke that perhaps she'd hopped on an earlier flight. There were no messages on my phone when I grabbed for it, so I made coffee for Leah and me and two soft-boiled eggs. On a whim I updated the Google doc—we'd actually never discussed it and over two years had passed since the booze cruise—but I emailed the updated link with Lake Vostok in Antarctica highlighted at the top. *We might not ever be able to see it, if we don't go soon,* I wrote in the message.

Almost immediately, my wife replied. *That's depressing. Maybe don't send me climate change shit this early in the morning. Anyhoo, plane delayed.*

*

I didn't have any evidence that Raquel was cheating on me as well, just a hunch, and part of me wished we could just sit down and have a conversation about it. We'd had such a gorgeous wedding. It seemed stupid to hold on to that, except that in front of all of your friends and family, isn't it real? Isn't it something?

After Raquel and I had come back from our honeymoon, things already felt changed. For me, un-fiancéd once and also divorced once,

I didn't care to start over once again. Raquel, she was hard to read, but we agreed to stay together. Or, we didn't make a move to split. I can say she seemed happier when I gave her space, and she seemed happier still when I was gone on business trips or vice versa. She'd be cheerful when I called from the road, or when she called me from the road, and then gloomy when we were together in person.

Her own work was progressing, in the non-profit space. Most of what she did was related to food deserts and job access, so I thought she would have appreciated my concern about the polar ice melting, Lake Vostok's banks turning to slush.

"I heard there is a commune around Nederland," she had told me recently.

Even early on, before Leah, sometimes instead of fucking, Raquel and I held hands in bed while her body curled around mine. As a man I didn't think I was supposed to admit it, but there were ways in that it was better than sex—her tits gently against my back, her fingers spread on my shoulders.

"I don't know that I want to go to a commune in Ned," I said. "That would be a long commute."

"The idea would not be to commute," Raquel said. "The idea would be to find a life there."

I bristled, without meaning too. Who would seriously want to live in a commune? Not me. Raquel unspooled her body from mine, just a millimeter or two but I felt it. I missed the narrow mattresses of our honeymoon, where the European beds were so slim, where when we were fighting there was nowhere to get away except the floor. At least then our fights had a stake in the ground, with one of us curled on the dirty carpet.

Her hair always smelled. Sometimes it was dirt from Burning Man's playa—the long expanse of inland dirt that was inspiring Raquel to ask for a different life—and sometimes it was chemical—the infusions that once kept Raquel rainbow-hued and now kept the gray from peeking in—and sometimes it was something I couldn't place—the smell of hope or fear or maybe even resignation.

*

I had taken a shower after fucking Leah one last time before Raquel got home, but I worried I looked too freshly showered so I did some yardwork. I had washed the sheets in the guestroom and then put them back on the bed, and I hoped the house didn't smell like laundry, because really I never touched the laundry except for the guest bed sheets. I went to the liquor store and purchased a bottle of tequila and poured what I hoped was the right amount down the drain. Raquel was very late from her flight, so I didn't have to worry about my cleaning smells after all, but just as I put my head on the pillow, my phone lit up with Leah.

u awake? her message read.

No, I tapped back.

chris u have 2 know the reason I luv u is bc ur so stupid not in spite of it

Yes, I replied.

whats the song u liked? leather smthg?

Leather and Lace

kinda weird title for a song, she said.

*

I thought I was being really careful, but I guess I wasn't. I'd been careful not to move things around in the laundry room, but when Raquel went to wash her travel clothes, she pulled out a wadded pair of underwear from the dryer that she did not recognize but that I certainly did.

"Really, Christian?" she said, waving the wad of lime green nylon in my face. "Really?"

She threw Leah's underwear in my face and that night I slept in the guestroom on new sheets, annoyed and wondering how Leah had left her underwear and equally annoyed that I hadn't double-checked the dryer.

I asked Raquel if she wanted to go to counseling, but she said she would rather move to the place she had been talking about in the mountains, the commune. Frankly I hadn't thought she'd been serious about that.

"One of the women from my old office," I said, "I think she grew up there. A bit less love and light and a whole lot more of crapping outside and making jam or some such. They killed their own animals. They made headcheese."

I wasn't entirely sure what headcheese was, but it sounded gross enough to maybe turn Raquel off to the idea.

"So?" Raquel said.

"Maybe you should talk to her," I said. "Maybe it wasn't that great."

"God, you really are depressing," she said.

"You also cheated on me," I said.

"I didn't," she said. "Made out a few times but stopped there."

"Do you want to divorce?" I asked, and the look she gave me was the same look Leah had given me—that she couldn't believe I was so stupid to ask, but I really did want to know the answer.

"I don't want to divorce," I whispered.

"No shit, Christian," she said.

*

I'm not sure if the counseling helped or not. It was a lot of work to talk Raquel into it, and ultimately, we did end up at the commune. Leah left for Hawaii right around the same time. We sold all of our furniture that was worth anything on Craigslist and the rest I gave to my cousin. He said he was on the cusp of splitting with his wife too and I begged him to come along with us, to make a fresh start like Raquel and I were doing. I said the community would welcome him. They were big on second chances.

He said he'd rather go at it alone, and I envied him once again, wishing it was just him and me, and a bottle of champagne.

At the commune, a place called The Circle, I rewired the few woodframed houses that were more like shanties and replaced the copper connections in an ancient telco box down by the end of the road so the one phone signal would at least be a little stronger. Raquel and I had sold our house at a loss and purchased a camper van. Then we put the van up on blocks to save the tires and started to live in a way that was very familiar to the commune, but was not familiar to us as first but started to make sense over time.

I was right that my old coworker Melissa was from the place. She didn't really want to talk to me, but she and Raquel struck up a passable friendship.

We worked together in the gardens, we put up food for the winter—like *animals*, I muttered under my breath, but I also found that what I knew about keeping old servers and computer hardware alive translated pretty well to dying farm equipment and busted up cars. Gears and motors whirring. So, I could lose myself in that, rebuilding a carburetor or replacing some hoses.

Our camper was a small, closed space, though we had many years where neither of us pulled away or slept on the floor. If I was being cynical I would say it was because there wasn't enough room to move around, or we were both too tired to move at the end of the day, but Raquel had been right about something about the commune, in that it drew us closer together, knitted us to one another in a way I hadn't felt in years.

Though Raquel got rid of hers, I did keep my cellphone, even though they were frowned upon. There was plenty of signal. The area was tucked at the end of a rural road, but there was a decent sized town nearby and line of sight to several cell towers, if you knew what to look for, so sometimes I'd still text Leah, but once she got to Hawaii, I stopped hearing from her, and that felt okay. Melissa, from my old office, said she was going to dig a new outhouse hole and that she had done it before. We dug and dug, and when we were done, I dropped the phone to the bottom of the pit. When I looked back, I realized I had forgotten to power it down, and there was a blue blinking light of a message hailing me from the dirt.

MORE TERRIBLE WAYS TO MAKE A LIVING

All through the winter, I stayed unemployed. I had a few interviews, each one a little more anxiety-making than the last—I'd stay up close to all night trying on different outfits and different hairstyles, struggling to understand what image I wanted to present. Young? Pulled together? Experienced but still hip? I worried that boots might come off as trying to look sexy, or an updo might seem too severe. Usually I defaulted to the same black tailored pants paired with a blouse that I hoped seemed normal-looking but hopefully also fun, purple with tiny birds on it. A jacket, even though I hated wearing jackets. Matte flats to match the blouse.

At the end of every interview, they asked, "What questions do you have for us?" and I recited the things I knew I was supposed to say, *How do you measure success in this position?* and *What would you ideally like to see me accomplish in the first 30-60-90 days?* but what I really wanted to say was, *Do you think you consider the capacity for kindness a measure of success?* and *Do you understand empathy as an ideal accomplishment?*

Maybe they read those other questions on my face, because I didn't get any offers. By the time spring had come, I was ready for a break in the cold, but it was Denver, where March and April are usually the months with the most precipitation, and there was still the possibility of extreme weather.

My money was starting to run out, and I was starting to feel nervous in a way I hadn't felt in a long time. At first it was just drawing down my savings; that was okay. That is what savings can be for. Then my unemployment insurance ended, and then I still had some lingering bills from my divorce, and then suddenly I was looking at numbers that were dangerously close to zeros.

Sometimes it was hard to remember what had felt so important about my ex-husband, Jimmy. The inhale and exhale of him. Like the elevator at my old job, going up, just to come back down—all the electricity and cabling and safety inspections it took to make it compliant, the hidden infrastructure meant to make life a little easier, when in fact the stairs worked just fine and gave us some time to think, and a reason to get our breath going, to make sure our hearts were working.

When a springtime blizzard hit, I hadn't prepared for it other than to fill up a couple of jugs of water. There was enough to make tea on the gas stove of my apartment and dip a washcloth into what was left of the hot water to wash my face, clean my pits, wipe my crotch. A couple of times, I drizzled water into an old box of mix to make pancakes that I seared in a pan and ate without butter or syrup or even peanut butter, because I was out of everything. It took three days for the power and water to come back on, but that was okay. The pancakes weren't amazing, but I wasn't freezing or starving. Mostly I just sat around, wrapped in a comforter. It was nice. I didn't have much to do anyway, but it was a good feeling to not be actively avoiding anything.

Before my phone died, I had a text ready to send to Jimmy, but just as I finished composing it, which took way longer than it should have, the screen blinked to black. Then I was glad for it, that I hadn't messaged him.

I hadn't bothered to go out to charge my phone or laptop at a coffee shop or somewhere else with a working outlet because I didn't have a lot of communication happening, and it was keeping me from texting Jimmy. Once I was all powered up and connected to the network, I was surprised to see that there was e-mail in my inbox, including a note from a company whom I'd met with so long ago I'd given up on them.

When the overhead light washed onto the dirty kitchen floors and filmy living room rug, instead of feeling grateful, I wondered what exactly I thought was going to happen and what I was going to see, besides my dirty apartment, illuminated.

Dear Katrina, they said, *We have considered your background, and based on our conversation with you, we think you are the right person to help our organization grow. Attached please find an offer letter to return at your convenience.*

I read the message three times, powered the phone back down, and turned off the lights. While I was sure I was supposed to be happy about this, I wasn't sure if I was. It wasn't the worst thing to work in an office. There were in fact many much more terrible ways to make a living.

Maybe the only thing I missed about Jimmy was having someone to bounce some ideas off of, and maybe the only thing I missed about my old office was that it was a distraction from Jimmy.

The text, which was still in my drafts, blinked. All it said was that I had paid the lawyer's final fee, which was not actually true, and that I had gotten the letter he had sent me, which was true but didn't change how I felt. I wanted to know if it would change how I felt if he replied, if we had a back-and-forth. An inhale after our exhale.

Part of me was excited about a new desk with new people and new ideas. Another part of me wanted to keep the lights off forever, and better yet, keep the power off forever, and just stay in a persistent state of half to full dark.

Yet in the morning, I made a cup of tea, got on my laptop instead of just scrolling my phone, and digitally signed the offer letter. Without work, I had too much time to examine my life, and way too much time to think about Jimmy. It was Thursday, and I filled out the paperwork for a drug test, a background check, and a credit evaluation. I didn't even have to talk to HR, since I'd been entered into the system, and the system gave me a timeline to pee in a cup, report any felonies or misdemeanors, and submit my social security number for verification. Outside of a fresh urine sample, I was sure they already had all my information, but I made the appointments and entered the data in the online interface anyway. I decided not to feel creeped by the algorithm's prediction that I had an 89 percent chance of passing my drug test, 70 percent (average, nothing to worry about) that I would check out in terms of credit and criminal history, and that my probability of retaining the job for more than two years was 73.5 percent based on those and other factors.

"WOULD YOU LIKE TO CONFIRM YOUR APPLICATION FOR KATRINA?" the screen blinked, displaying *Yes, No,* or *Go Back* options.

Yes. I clicked the green button, but nothing happened.

I clicked again, but again, nothing. I wondered if I had waited too long and my application had expired, even though the date on the offer letter was still within range.

My laptop was newer and had a touch screen that I barely used unless the mouse was frozen, but now I jabbed at the green button, fingertip to polarized glass, stabbing at the *Yes* while the interface did not respond. I let it sit for a minute while I got a glass of ice water, and clicked again. This time it went through and I was directed to the confirmation screen. "GOOD LUCK," it read in bright-green letters just as my phone dinged with a confirmation message.

I deleted the system text, and then sent a new one to Jimmy. *Still unemployed,* I wrote, *any chance you could take the rest of the divorce bill if you are working?*

Sure, he replied. *Not a prob. Should have offered. Knew you were in a tough spot. Get my letter?*

No! I wrote. *You sent something?!*

Don't worry about it, he wrote. *I don't remember what I put in there anyway.* Ha.

Haha, I tapped on the little screen. *Maybe for the best.*

After that, he didn't reply. I ate the last dry pancake and made another cup of tea, drank another glass of ice water. Hot and cold.

The algorithms, really, didn't keep me up at night, though I wondered what a few days without data input, like when the power was off, would do or had done, and I wondered if Jimmy and I could have been predicted. I might have married him anyway.

People say all the time that we only have one life, and they say to live our best life, but outside of clicky content or taking off to an ashram, the specifics, at least to me, seemed pretty thin. There was one time, just before things got really bad with Jimmy, that we had a momentary break in the tension, and one evening he made dinner and I cleaned up the kitchen, and we both took a glass of wine out to the front porch and watched the people of our neighborhood go by on their evening walks and bike rides. Across the street, a man whose name we didn't know was getting out of his car with a vase of flowers and he dropped the whole thing, and the roses and lilies and what looked to me like spider mums sprayed across the driveway, broken glass glittering and the water spreading into a dark spot.

Jimmy laughed and said that the guy was now in bigger trouble than whatever had prompted him to buy flowers in the first place.

"We're all in bigger trouble," I had said. I had a stash of vases under the sink in the laundry room, but I didn't move to get the guy a new one, though I easily could have.

Instead, we watched him pick up the stems and then the glass, and then we went inside. What would have changed if I'd left the porch— shown the guy some kindness, disrupted the loop that Jimmy and I were in? It might have saved us all.

ABOUT THE AUTHOR

Wendy J. Fox is the author of four books of fiction. Her novel *If the Ice Had Held* was named a best read by *Buzzfeed, High Country News*, Westword, and LitHub (audio), and she has been a finalist for the Colorado Book Award twice. A frequent contributor to national publications, she has written for *Self, Business Insider, Ms. Magazine, Buzzfeed News* and others. She has also written for literary sites including *The Millions, The Rumpus*, and *Electric Literature*.

Also from Wendy J. Fox

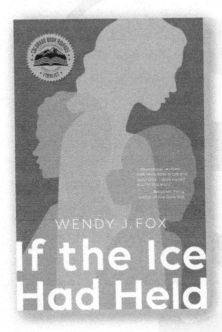

"Razor-sharp…written with incredible grace and assurance. I gave myself over to this story and felt as though I had inhabited these characters."
— Benjamin Percy, author of *The Dark Net*

I found it nearly impossible to put this book down."
— Small Press Picks

"A terrific novel [that] weaves several different stories, across a span of time, and it all culminates in one of the best final chapters I've read in a novel in a long time."
— David Abrams, founder, *The Quivering Pen*
